The Adventure of the Detected Detective

Recent Titles in
Contributions to the Study of World Literature

Catholic Fiction and Social Reality in Ireland, 1873–1922
James H. Murphy

A Morbid Fascination: White Prose and Politics in Apartheid South Africa
Richard Peck

The Other Mirror: Women's Narrative in Mexico, 1980–1995
Kristine Ibsen, editor

Searching for Recognition: The Promotion of Latin American Literature in the United States
Irene Rostagno

James Merrill's Poetic Quest
Don Adams

Sounding the Classics: From Sophocles to Thomas Mann
Rudolph Binion

Homeric Rhythm: A Philosophical Study
Paolo Vivante

Virginia Woolf: Feminism, Creativity, and the Unconscious
John R. Maze

The French Revolution Debate in English Literature and Culture
Lisa Plummer Crafton, editor

Jane Austen and Eighteenth-Century Courtesy Books
Penelope Joan Fritzer

James Joyce and Trieste
Peter Hartshorn

True Relations: Essays on Autobiography and the Postmodern
G. Thomas Couser and Joseph Fichtelberg, editors

The Adventure of the Detected Detective

Sherlock Holmes in James Joyce's *Finnegans Wake*

WILLIAM D. JENKINS

Contributions to the Study of World Literature,
Number 54

Greenwood Press
Westport, Connecticut • London

Library of Congress Cataloging-in-Publication Data

Jenkins, William D., 1916–
The adventure of the detected detective : Sherlock Holmes in James Joyce's Finnegans wake / William D. Jenkins.
p. cm.—(Contributions to the study of world literature, ISSN 0738–9345 ; no. 54)
Includes bibliographical references and index.
ISBN 0–313–29143–8
1. Joyce, James, 1882–1941. Finnegans wake. 2. Detective and mystery stories, English—Appreciation. 3. Doyle, Arthur Conan, Sir, 1859–1930—Influence. 4. Joyce, James, 1882–1941—Knowledge—Literature. 5. Holmes, Sherlock (Fictitious character) 6. Private investigators in literature. I. Title. II. Series.
PR6019.O9F59355 1998
823′.912—dc20 93–21144

British Library Cataloguing in Publication Data is available.

Library of Congress Catalog Card Number: 93–21144
ISBN: 0–313–29143–8
ISSN: 0738–9345

First published in 1998

Greenwood Press, 88 Post Road West, Westport, CT 06881
An imprint of Greenwood Publishing Group, Inc.

Printed in the United States of America

The paper used in this book complies with the Permanent Paper Standard issued by the National Information Standards Organization (Z39.48–1984).

10 9 8 7 6 5 4 3 2 1

The figure on page 48 is from "The Dancing Men," in *The Later Adventures of Sherlock Holmes* (New York: Heritage Press, 1952), 822.

Copyright Acknowledgments

In memory

William David Jenkins,

husband, father, gentleman, scholar, soldier, and friend

Contents

Preface

"You don't know about me without you have read a book by the name of *The Adventures of Tom Sawyer*; but that ain't no matter." So begins the Greatest American Novel.

You won't know about *Finnegans Wake* without you have read books by the names of *Dubliners, Stephen Hero, A Portrait of the Artist as a Young Man, Ulysses*; but that ain't no matter either. Undeniably, the works of James Joyce develop in breadth, depth and complexity, sequentially as they were written. But one can, if one chooses, start with any one of the books and read it with pleasure. Indeed, in the case of *Finnegans Wake*, you can start anywhere toward the middle and read all the way around back to your starting point, because that's one way it was intended to be read. So familiarity with Joyce's earlier work is helpful in reading the *Wake*, but the important reading prerequisite is not selectivity, nor even quality, as much as it is quantity.

We may assume that any person who has read English literature in any quantity at the high school level has read most, if not all, of Arthur Conan Doyle's Sherlock Holmes stories. Such readers need not be excessively intimidated by *Finnegans Wake*. If they enjoy the traditional author-reader contest of the detective story, they will discover the *Wake* offers the familiar challenge in an unfamiliar form. They will discover that *Finnegans Wake* is, among other things, the greatest whodunit ever written. "The keys to. Given!" says Joyce.

The adventures of Sherlock Holmes, probably the most popular and readable body of literary work ever written in any language, may provide a key to one of the most abstruse and demanding works ever written in any language. In detecting and explicating these allusions to the world's greatest detective, it is my expectation that, as readers achieve more understanding of *Finnegans Wake*, they may be inspired to explore the numerous passages leading away from Sherlock Holmes to other sources. Reading the *Wake* is a most amusing and edifying game.

According to Frank Budgen, Joyce "regarded the English interest in crime in the shape of the detective story as exceptionally ludicrous, and considered the English ... prone to thoughts of crime."[1] It is certainly true that there is much of the burlesque in Joyce's treatment of Sherlock Holmes. Perhaps Holmes is even "exceptionally" burlesqued, although in *Finnegans Wake* no hero is entirely untouched by mockery, not excepting Joyce himself. Be that as it may, aficionados of Sherlock Holmes may also derive greater insight and appreciation of the Master by seeing him through Joyce's eyes.

In my single-minded pursuit of Sherlockiana through the pages of the *Wake*, I have undoubtedly made many interpretations that are overly imaginative or based on faulty reasoning and ignorant assumptions. Readers are therefore reminded that *Wake* explication, in the words of the old Irish joke, "is not a private fight. Annybody can jine in." To which the *Wake* adds, "with the shoutmost shoviality." And although I have tried to emulate the Master's thoroughness, there is no reason to suppose that every Sherlockian allusion in the *Wake* is contained herein. (Where is *A Study in Scarlet*?) Come, Watsons, come! The game's afoot!

A special expression of thanks must be made to Adeline Glasheen, author of *A Census of Finnegans Wake* (1963). To this study Mrs. Glasheen has provided innumerable items of straight information as well as many heuristic ideas and indirect clues.

NOTE

Jane Jenkins would like to thank her late husband's dear friend, Mr. Avery Lackner, for all his wonderful help and advice in preparing this book for publication.

1. Frank Budgen, *James Joyce and the Making of Ulysses* (Oxford: University Press, 1972), 191.

The Adventure of the Detected Detective

Chapter 1

It Seems There Were Two Irishmen ... Doyle and Joyce

"Even today, despite her heavy obstacles, Ireland is making her contribution to English art and thought,"[1] observed James Joyce in a lecture in Trieste, April 1907. He went on to name FitzGerald, Burton, Cary, Sir Arthur Sullivan, Edward O'Connor, George Moore, Shaw and Wilde as men of Irish ancestry whose work constituted "an intellectual oasis in the Sahara of false spiritualistic, Messianic, and detective writings whose name is legion in England." Unfortunately for Joyce's thesis, his contempt for spiritualistic and detective writings pointed directly at one who was "all too Irish,"[2] Sir Arthur Conan Doyle, then at the apex of his popularity. And ironically, Joyce's phrase "intellectual oasis in the Sahara of ... detective writings" seems to have been borrowed from the older Irishman. In Doyle's *The Sign of the Four* (1890), Thaddeus Sholto describes his house as "an oasis of art in the howling desert of South London." Although born in Scotland (FitzGerald, Burton and Sullivan were born in England), Doyle was solidly Irish—and from an Irish Catholic family at that. His grandfather was an Irish painter who emigrated; his mother was a Foley of County Waterford.

Among all the commentators on Joyce, only Hugh Kenner has made a comparison with the works of Doyle. In the essay "Baker Street to Eccles Street," it is Kenner's theme that the Sherlock Holmes–Dr. Watson relationship has a certain correspondence to the Stephen Dedalus–Leopold Bloom relationship.[3] As will be shown, there are many more correspondences, and some evidence indicates that Joyce occasionally drew on Doyle as a source. Since Doyle himself undervalued his Sherlock Holmes stories, he might well have accepted Kenner's characterization of them as "subaesthetic." But

Kenner's broad characterization of Doyle as "a Bloom writing for Blooms" does less than complete justice to a complex individual who was capable on occasion of burning with a hard Shem-like flame. Doyle battled the British Home Office for years over the unjust conviction of a discriminated-against Parsi, George Edalji. He waged a similar fight on behalf of Oscar Slater, a German Jew unjustly convicted of murder. He warmly espoused the unconventional cause of spiritualism and pleaded in wartime for the life of Roger Casement. In these quarrels and many others, Doyle engaged at various times the clergy, the press, the military, the law and officialdom in general, writing in the same spirit of scornful fire that Joyce used in his own occasional polemics.

In January 1907, Doyle launched his newspaper and pamphlet campaign to clear the name of George Edalji, and in September of the same year Joyce was moved to add his own comment. He concluded an essay on English injustice toward Ireland, written for a Trieste newspaper, with an allusion to the Edalji case: "At Great Wyrely in England ... bestial, maddened criminals have ravaged the cattle to such an extent that the English companies will no longer insure them. Five years ago an innocent man, now at liberty, was condemned to forced labour to appease public indignation."[4] To have given credit to Doyle as the Irishman fighting for the innocent man (vide Dreyfus and Zola) might have helped the young Joyce make a point with this reference which otherwise seems petulantly irrelevant. However a combined allusion to Sherlock Holmes and Oscar Slater in *Finnegans Wake* may indicate that the mature Joyce took a more appreciative view of both Doyle and his detective: (*FW* 165.32–36) "I should like to ask that Shedlock Holmes person who is out for removing the roofs of our criminal classics by what *deductio ad domunum* he hopes *de tacto* to detect anything unless he happens himself *movibile tectu* to have a slade off." Doyle revealed the scandalous facts, removed the lid (*movibile tectu*) and got Slater off (slade off). In a letter of thanks, Slater addressed Doyle as the "breaker of my shackles"[5] (Shedlock). Slater had been prejudged as guilty *ad hominem* (*deductio ad domunum*). The alleged murder weapon was a tack hammer (*de tacto*).[6] As for Sherlock Holmes, he raised the literary level of the detective story (removed the roofs of our criminal classics).

An example of prose that Joyce should have appreciated occurs in "The Adventure of the Three Students," wherein Holmes says to Watson: "By Jove! my dear fellow, it is nearly nine, and the landlady babbled of green peas at seven-thirty." The subtlety of the parody on *Henry V*, II, iii, is such that it invokes not only the speech, but the speaker, Mistress Quickly. Joyce alludes to the same speech in *Finnegans Wake* (*FW* 10.34–35) "A verytableand of bleakbardfields! Under his seven wrothschields lies one Lumproar." Joyce's use of "table" for "babbled" is justified by the Shakespeare Folios, where the line reads "... and a Table of greene fields." "Lumproar" is, in part, Falstaff, who "fumbled with the sheets" and died like "any christom child." (Cf. the Jewish child, "wrothschields.")

And from Chapter 5 of Doyle's *The Lost World*: "So looks the Shakespearean who is confronted by a rancid Baconian." There is a close analogy in *Ulysses* (U 195): "Good Bacon: gone musty. Shakespeare Bacon's wild oats." Oddly enough, this particular idea does not recur in *FW*, where Bacon is one of the favorite subjects for punning purposes. It is noteworthy that both of Doyle's puns are Shakespearean. As Matthew Hodgart has commented, in Joyce's use of puns he claimed "Shakespeare's punning as a precedent."[7]

Pride of lineage constitutes another correspondence among Shakespeare, Joyce and Doyle. Richard Ellmann points out that "James Joyce, like his father or, for that matter, like Shakespeare, took excellent care of the coat of arms."[8] Doyle's mother traced her family back through the Percys to King Henry III and required her son to study heraldry. But while Doyle might have said with Mr. Deasy in *Ulysses* (*U* 31), "We are all Irish, all kings' sons," he might also have added with Stephen Dedalus, "Alas." The similarity of backgrounds between the young Doyle and the young Joyce is striking.

Arthur Conan Doyle was the elder son in the large family of an impoverished civil servant. By scraping, the family managed to provide him with a fine classical education at Jesuit institutions, first at Hodder House School and then at Stonyhurst College in Lancashire. Young Doyle became the favorite of the masters, and the Stonyhurst Jesuits suggested to Mrs. Doyle that Arthur's tuition fees could be remitted if she would dedicate him to the church. Although the offer was rejected, the fathers remained hopeful. From all the students in his class they selected Doyle for advanced schooling at the Jesuit College of Feldkirch in Austria. Following his year at Feldkirch Doyle elected to study medicine at the University of Edinburgh. At the age of twenty-three, in 1882, the year Joyce was born, Doyle repudiated the church and adopted an agnostic position.

Similarly, James Joyce was the elder son in the large family of an impoverished civil servant. By scraping, the family managed to provide him with a fine classical education at Jesuit institutions, first at Clongowes Wood College in County Kildare and then at Belvedere College and University College, Dublin. At Belvedere young Joyce became the favorite of the Jesuit masters, who urged him to enter the priesthood. Instead, Joyce elected to study medicine at the University of Paris, later abandoning both Catholicism and medicine for literature.

At the University of Edinburgh Doyle made the acquaintance of a student named George Budd, who played an important role in his early life. Budd appears in Doyle's *Bildungsroman*, *The Stark-Munro Letters,* under the name "Cullingworth." Similarly, James Joyce on his return from Paris made the acquaintance of Oliver St. John Gogarty, who appears in *Ulysses* under the name "Buck Mulligan." The following characteristics of Budd-Cullingworth and his relationship to Doyle apply equally in fact and/or fiction to Gogarty-Mulligan and his relationship with Joyce.

- Budd-Cullingworth was a medical student when Doyle first knew him.
- Budd-Cullingworth was a wencher, drinker, braggart, raconteur, wit and unscrupulous liar.
- Budd-Cullingworth was physically strong, athletic and inclined to brutality.
- Budd-Cullingworth and Doyle lived together for a time.
- Budd-Cullingworth's friendship with Doyle was objectionable to the latter's parents.
- Budd-Cullingworth and Doyle quarreled over a misunderstanding involving Doyle's mother.
- Budd-Cullingworth exploited, patronized and eventually betrayed Doyle.
- The name "Budd-Cullingworth" even sounds like "Buck Mulligan."

For a confirming clue linking Budd-Cullingworth to Joyce, we are indebted to Hesketh Pearson. In his biography of Doyle, Pearson cites a passage from *The Land of Mist*, wherein Doyle's science fiction hero, Professor Challenger, attends a seance:

... when Challenger, in *The Land of Mist*, goes to a seance in order to expose the proceedings, the medium asks whether anyone present would own to a friend named Budworth, which is a combination of Budd and Cullingworth, the pseudonym invented by Doyle for Budd in *The Stark-Munro Letters* and retained by him in the story of his own life. No, reports the chronicler in *The Land of Mist*, 'no one would own to a friend named Budworth'—a casual comment, the true significance of which was lost on Doyle, who never recognized how much he owed as a story-teller to Budd.[9]

If it was in character for Doyle to fail to recognize a literary debt, it may have been equally in character for Joyce to acknowledge in *Finnegans Wake* a literary debt incurred in writing *Ulysses*. James S. Atherton has noted that Chapters 4 and 10 of *The Land of Mist* provide source material for pages 481–500 of *Finnegans Wake*.[10] Atherton has the right book, but not all the right chapters. The incident cited by Pearson is from Chapter 16 and appears in (*FW* 498.8–499.3):

... the houses of Orange and Betters M. P. ... out of their boom companions in paunchjab and dogril and pammel and gougerotty ... socializing and communicating in the deification of his members ... the poohpooher old bolssloose, with his arthurious clayroses ... on the table round, with the floodlight switched back ... and one by one tilly tallows round in ringcampf, circumassembled by his daughters in the foregiftness of his sons ... with a hogo, fluorescent of his swathings, round him ... with his buttend up, expositoed for sale after referee's inspection, bulgy and blowrious, bunged to ignorious, healed, cured and embalsamate, pending a rouseruction of his bogey, most highly astounded, as it turned up, after his life overlasting, at thus being reduced to nothing.[11]

The identification of this passage with a seance seems clear. The seance in Chapter 16 of *The Land of Mist* was conducted at London's Psychic College in Holland Park (houses of Orange), a place previously described by Doyle (Chapter 5) as a great "leveller of classes" where "the charwoman with psychic force is the superior of the millionaire who lacks it" (and Betters M.P.). The "poohpooher" is the skeptical Professor Challenger and "old bolssloose" is Mr. Bolsover, one of the true believers. Challenger was persuaded to attend the seance by his daughter (circumassembled by his daughters). The medium emerges from a cabinet wrapped in "an ectoplasmic covering" (with a hogo, fluorescent of his swathings, round him) and is promptly tackled by a professional football player whom Challenger had brought along for that very purpose, having previously searched the medium and his cabinet (after referee's inspection).

But the significant words are "gougerotty," "buttend up," "boom companions." The first seems to be the only *Finnegans Wake* reference to Gogarty by name. The next, "buttend up," not only means "Budworth," who was "expositoed for sale ... bunged to ignorious ... reduced to nothing," but also seems to imply that Joyce knew "Budworth" to be compounded of two names (with the "Budd" end up). As for "boom companions," it should be remembered that in *Ulysses* (*U* 647–48), "Boom" is a symbol of humiliating anonymity. The newspaper list of the mourners at Paddy Dignam's funeral includes "L. Boom," not "Bloom." Both Doyle and Budd-Cullingworth were boxing enthusiasts (companions in paunchjab and pammel ... ringcampf). The description "bulgy and blowrious" applies equally to "stately plump Buck Mulligan" as to Budd-Cullingworth. Note further that these words, followed by "bunged to ignorious" suggest "God Save the King." This may have some relevance to Doyle as discussed below.

If there is an analogy between Budd-Cullingworth and anybody in *Ulysses*, it is not a simple one-to-one correspondence. An entirely harmonious complexity is provided by the Englishman Haines, the third occupant of the Martello Tower. On (*U* 16) Haines says to Stephen: "I intend to make a collection of your sayings if you will let me." In Chapter 7 of *The Stark-Munro Letters* the Englishman Munro says of Cullingworth, "His conversation when he does not fly off at a tangent is full of pith and idea....He shoots off a whole collection of aphorisms in a single evening. I should like to have a man with a notebook always beside him to gather up his waste."

Doyle may also have provided a key phrase for Stephen's interior monologue of politically motivated resentment directed at Haines. Through the years Doyle's opinions on the Irish question changed, but in 1886 he was a Liberal-Unionist opposed to Home Rule. In his autobiography Doyle cites a newspaper report of a political speech he made in that year: "England and Ireland are wedded together with the sapphire wedding ring of the sea, and what God has placed together let no man pluck asunder."[12] On (*U* 186), wherein the thoughts of Stephen returned briefly to his morning conversation with Haines:

"We feel in England. Penitent thief. Gone. I smoked his baccy. Green twinkling stone. An emerald set in the ring of the sea."

Written in 1894, while the author was exiled in Switzerland because of his wife's ill health, *The Stark-Munro Letters* might well have been subtitled "A Portrait of Doyle as a Young Man." The book has been described by John Dickson Carr as "no 'story,' as he was known to do a story, but largely autobiographical ... a study of the thoughts, hopes, feelings, and above all, religious doubts of a young doctor."[13] Carr quotes Doyle's assessment of the book: " 'I cannot imagine what its value is. It will make a religious sensation if not a literary.' " The closer Joycean analogy is his first-draft *Stephen Hero* rather than the rewritten version, *A Portrait of the Artist as a Young Man*. Chapter 12 of *Stark-Munro* is largely devoted to a colloquy with a High Church curate:

> "Such a row we had!
>
> 'He [Jesus] triumphed over sin,' said my visitor, as if a text or a phrase were an argument.
>
> 'A cheap triumph!' I said. 'You remember that Roman emperor who used to descend into the arena fully armed, and pit himself against some poor wretch who had only a leaden foil which would double up at a thrust. According to your theory of your Master's life, you would have it that he faced the temptations of this world at such an advantage that they were only harmless leaden things, and not the sharp assailants that we find them... I don't pretend to know what truth is, for it is infinite and I am finite; but I know perfectly well what it is *not*.'
>
> 'You have evolved all this from your own spiritual pride and self-sufficiency,' said he hotly. 'Why do you not turn to that Deity whose name you use? Why do you not humble yourself before Him?' "

The argument between Stephen and Mrs. Dedalus in *Stephen Hero* follows a similar pattern and concludes on precisely the same note: "I know what is wrong with you—you suffer from the pride of the intellect. You forget that we are only worms of the earth. You think that you can defy God because you have misused the talents he has given you."[14]

William York Tindall has commented that in the "Ithaca" episode of *Ulysses* (*U* 708–9), "Bloom's library contains several significant volumes, *The Hidden Life of Christ* (black boards), for example, and *Plain Elements of Geometry*. Geometry is measuring the earth

(Molly)."[15] Also included is a copy of "*The Stark-Munro Letters* by A. Conan Doyle, property of the City of Dublin Public Library, 106 Capel Street, lent 21 May (Whitsun Eve) 1904, due 4 June 1904, 13 days overdue (black cloth binding, bearing white letter-number ticket)." Whitsunday commemorates the inspiration of the apostles by the Holy Spirit. Is there a hint here of an inspiration provided by the library book? And since the borrowed book is overdue, does it suggest that a debt of some sort has been acknowledged?

The hypothesis is strengthened by considerations of another possibly significant volume in addition to the two noted by Tindall, "*Laurence Bloomfield in Ireland* ... previous owner's name on recto of flyleaf erased." And while reading the various titles, Bloom reflects on "the insecurity of hiding any secret document behind, beneath, or between the pages of a book."

Primarily the words "secret document" constitute one of the final enigmatic references to Bloom's erotic correspondence with Martha Clifford, which first appear on (*U* 56): "He peeped quickly inside the leather headband. White slip of paper. Quite safe." Twenty pages later the slip of paper is identified, making this one of the simpler enigmatic references in *Ulysses*. Another early enigmatic reference is to *The Stark-Munro Letters*. (*U* 64–65) "Must get that Capel street library book renewed or they'll write to Kearney, my guarantor. Reincarnation, that's the word.... Some say they remember their past lives." At first reading, the word "reincarnation" here seems to be merely a synonym for "metempsychosis," which Bloom has been explaining to Molly. However, I suggest that in this context "reincarnation" has a double meaning: *Ulysses* itself is, in some respects, a reincarnation of *The Stark-Munro Letters*.

And *The Stark-Munro Letters* also provides us with an echo of Joyce's *A Portrait of the Artist as a Young Man*. Writes Doyle:

> I have often wondered why some of those writing fellows don't try their hands at drawing the inner life of a young man from about the age of puberty until he begins to find his feet a little. Men are very fond of analysing the feelings of their heroines, which they cannot possibly know anything about, while they have little to say of the inner development of their heroes, which is an experience which they have themselves undergone... but since ... I am convinced that it is the common lot. The shrinking, horrible shy-

ness, alternating with occasional absurd fits of audacity which represent the reaction against it, the longing for close friendship, the agonies over imaginary slights, the extraordinary sexual doubts, the deadly fears caused by non-existent diseases, the vague emotion produced by all women, and the half-frightened thrill by particular ones, the aggressiveness caused by fear of being afraid, the sudden blacknesses, the profound self-distrust—I dare bet that you have felt every one of them Bertie, just as I have, and that the first lad of eighteen whom you see out of your window is suffering from them now.[16]

Note Doyle's opinion that writers are "very fond of analysing the feelings of their heroines, which they cannot possibly know anything about." This opinion was shared by Nora Joyce, who said of her husband, "He knew nothing about women."[17]

Elsewhere in *Stark-Munro* we find Doyle espousing a philosophy similar to that of Giordano Bruno, whose doctrine of the unity of opposites greatly influenced Joyce. Said Doyle:

In this world, however, part of the beautiful poise of things depends upon the fact that whenever you have an exaggerated fanatic of any sort, his exact opposite springs up to neutralize him. You have a Mameluke: up jumps a Crusader. You have a Fenian: up jumps an Orangeman. Every force has its recoil. And so these more hidebound scientists must be set against those gentlemen who still believe that the world was created in the year 4004 BC.[18]

Joyce's use of the enigmatic reference has been the subject of much scholarly comment, most of it concerned with the repetition of specific phrases, words or sounds. The technique is said to derive ultimately from the Wagnerian leitmotiv. But considered at another level, Joyce's enigmatic reference is not unlike the technique of the enigmatic clue which was invented by Arthur Conan Doyle. Carr discusses two classic examples of the device, "the curious incident of the dog in the night-time," from "Silver Blaze," and the missing dumbbell from *The Valley of Fear*. " 'Dear me, Watson, is it possible that you have not penetrated the fact that the case hangs upon the missing dumb-bell?' Holmes goes on and on about it until both Watson and the reader become desperate. What is the meaning of the dumbbell? What enormous significance is attached to Watson's umbrella?"[19]

The device employed in "The Oxen of the Sun" episode in *Ulysses* has also been much admired. By means of style parodies, from Anglo-Saxon chronicles through Malory and Carlyle to twentieth-century slang, Joyce carries the thread of a single narrative while depicting the development of English literature. The result might be called a literary mosaic. Stuart Gilbert identifies the technique of the episode as "Embryonic Development."[20] If the technique itself had an embryo, perhaps it may be found in one of Doyle's earliest (1886) short stories, "Cyprian Overbeck Wells: A Literary Mosaic."[21] Like Stephen Dedalus, Doyle's hero is an unsuccessful young writer who seeks inspiration in "the works of the leading English novelists, from Daniel Defoe to the present day in the hope of stimulating my latent ideas and getting a good grasp of the general tendency of literature." Fatigued by hours of such study, "on the night of the fourth of June, eighteen hundred and eighty six," the hero falls asleep and dreams that he is visited by the shades of "the greatest masters of fiction in every age of English letters," who agree to construct a story, each contributing in turn. Gilbert has noted the styles of Defoe and Swift in "The Oxen of the Sun." Doyle also parodies these two as well as Smollett, Scott and Bulwer-Lytton. On a certain passage (*U* 412) in "The Oxen of the Sun" Gilbert comments ambiguously, "shades of *The Castle of Otranto*." Tindall, even more noncommittal, calls it "a parody of the Gothic novel."[22] Horace Walpole's *The Castle of Otranto* is generally accepted as the prototype of all Gothic tales. Nevertheless, it is suggested here that the *Ulysses* passage is primarily Bulwer-Lytton cum Doyle.

Doyle was indisputably a master of the Gothic genre, and "Cyprian Overbeck Wells" might be described as comic Gothic. As for direct textual correspondence:

• Here is a sentence from "The Haunted and the Haunters" by Bulwer-Lytton: "The closet door to the right of the fireplace now opened, and from the aperture there came the form of an aged woman."[23]

• From "Cyprian Overbeck Wells," Doyle's parody of Bulwer-Lytton: "... a secret door opened and a venerable old man swept majestically into the apartment."

• From "The Oxen of the Sun" (*U* 412), Joyce's parody of Doyle's parody of Bulwer-Lytton: "The secret panel beside the chimney slid back and in the recess appeared ... Haines!"

Note that Buck Mulligan is the narrator of Joyce's Gothic passage. "The sage repeated *Lex talionis*. The sentimentalist is he who would enjoy without incurring the immense debtorship for a thing done. Malachias, overcome by emotion, ceased. The mystery was unveiled. Haines was the third brother. His real name was Childs."[24]

Doyle's dreaming writer is awakened, and the story of "Cyprian Overbeck Wells" remains unfinished. "But I still live in the hopes that in some future dream the great masters may themselves finish what they have begun," wrote Doyle in 1886. That James Joyce finished it in 1921 is strongly suggested by the day and month of the dream of "Cyprian Overbeck Wells." It was "the fourth of June," the same date in 1904 that the copy of *The Stark-Munro Letters* was due back at the Capel Street Library. Ellmann has pointed out that "inspired cribbing was always part of Joyce's talent. His gift was for transforming material, not originating it ... As [Joyce] once said to Frank Budgen, 'Have you ever noticed when you get an idea, how much *I* can make of it?' "[25]

NOTES

1. James Joyce, "Ireland, Land of Saints and Sages," *The Critical Writings,* ed. Ellsworth Mason and Richard Ellmann (New York: Viking Press, 1964), 171.

2. Joyce, *Ulysses* (reprint, New York, Random House/Modern Library, 1961), 623. Stephen Dedalus is thinking of his father's overrich endowment in the national characteristics, and he is probably quoting the concluding paragraph of Thomas Carlyle's *Sartor Resartus*. All *Ulysses* page numbers refer to this edition.

3. Hugh Kenner, *Dublin's Joyce* (Boston: Beacon Press, 1962), 158–178.

4. James Joyce, "Ireland at the Bar," in *Critical Writings*, 200.

5. Quoted by Pierre Nordon, *Conan Doyle: A Biography* (New York: Holt, Rhinehart and Winston, 1964), 171.

6. See also *Finnegans Wake* (FW 511.4): "With Slater's hammer perhaps?"

7. Matthew J. C. Hodgart, "Shakespeare and *Finnegans Wake*," *The Cambridge Journal*, 6 (September 1953), 735–752.

8. Richard Ellmann, *James Joyce* (New York: Oxford University Press, 1959), 9–10.

9. Kesketh Pearson, *Conan Doyle* (New York, 1960), 247.

10. James S. Atherton, *The Books at the Wake* (New York: Viking Press, 1960), 247.

11. Joyce's remarkable familiarity with Doyle's work is indicated by a sentence occurring two pages later (FW 501.13–14): "Challenger's Deep is childsplay to this but, by our soundings in the swish channels, land is due." The allusion combines Professor Challenger with *The Maracot Deep*, a novel of submarine exploration. Nordon points out that Challenger and Maracot are interchangeable science-fiction heroes.

12. Arthur Conan Doyle, *Memories and Adventures* (Boston: Little, Brown, 1924), 86. This autobiography could not have been a source for anything in *Ulysses*. But Doyle had been a famous man for decades, and his public statements on all subjects were well known.

13. John Dickson Carr, *The Life of Sir Arthur Conan Doyle* (New York: Harper and Brothers, 1949), 80.

14. James Joyce, *Stephen Hero* (reprint, Norfolk, Conn.: New Directions, 1963), 134.

15. William York Tindall, *A Reader's Guide to James Joyce* (New York, 1964), 230.

16. Arthur Conan Doyle, *The Stark-Munro Letters* (New York: D. Appleton & Co., 1895), 56–7.

17. Reported by Samuel Beckett in Ellmann, *Joyce*, 642.

18. Doyle, *Stark-Munro*, 312–313.

19. Carr, *Doyle*, 234.

20. Stuart Gilbert, *James Joyce's Ulysses* (New York: Modern Library, 1952), 295–312.

21. Arthur Conan Doyle, "Cyprian Overbeck Wells," in *Conan Doyle's Best Books* Vol. I, (New York: P.F. Collier & Son, n.d.), 327–354.

22. Tindall, *Reader's Guide*, 202.

23. Edward Bulwer-Lytton, "The Haunted and the Haunters," in *Famous Ghost Stories*, (New York: Illustrated Modern Library, 1944), 24.

24. In October 1899 a Dublin court acquitted Samuel Childs of the murder of his brother Thomas. (See Ellmann, 95–96, 767.) There are many allusions in *Ulysses* to the Childs murder case, but this is the only one involving Haines. Why did Joyce confuse the name of the innocent accused with that of the murder victim? "I am the murderer of Samuel Childs (sic)."

25. Richard Ellmann, introduction to Stanislaus Joyce, *My Brother's Keeper* (New York: Viking Press, 1958), xv.

Chapter 2

Sigersons Wake

Let us consider the implication of a remark made by Sherlock Holmes to Watson in *The Adventure of the Empty House*. "You may have read of the remarkable explorations of a Norwegian named Sigerson, but I am sure it never occurred to you that you were receiving news of your friend."

That single sentence functions as a type of Rosetta Stone in detecting allusions to Sherlock Holmes in *Finnegans Wake*. Whenever we see the name "Sigerson" in however distorted a form, we know we are receiving news of our friend. In *FW* the genius of Baker Street is frequently concealed in the words "home," "homely" and similar cognates. But he makes his first appearance as "Comestipple Sacksoun" on page 15 and as "Sigerson" on page 608, twenty pages before the last. In intervening passages he is called "the Sockerson boy," "comestabulish Sigurdson," "Seckesign," "Sickerson," "Seckerson," "Sackerson," "pollysigh patrolman Seckersenn" as well as perhaps a score of aliases we hope to elucidate in the course of our investigation. We shall see him as Basil, Lally, Cox and Jute. Although he shares the identity of the Norwegian captain, other claimants seem secondary. He is sometimes Shem and sometimes Finn MacCool, the heroic giant of Irish myth.

Watson is mentioned in *FW* once by name. He is also Box and Mutt, and may be identified sometimes with Shaun. In the Irish legend Finn MacCool had an implacable enemy named Goll. Finn killed Goll and was in turn killed by Goll's henchmen. Thus, Professor Moriarty, Colonel Sebastian Moran and some of the other criminal opponents of Holmes may be Goll and his henchmen, gillies, gollies, jollys and other variants.

Holmes had a rare talent which made him especially worthy of attention in *FW*. He was an expert at reading codes and cyphers, and *FW* itself is a cryptogram written in an invented language called "Djoytsch." Basically English, it employs bits and "etyms" of words from as many foreign languages as the Irish polyglot could include. Furthermore, they are frequently compounded like Lewis Carroll's "portmanteau" words. Hence, for convenient reference, citations of passages from *FW* are identified by page and line number like this: (324.21), which means page 324 line 21: "Ellers for the greeter glossary of code, callen hom" (All for the greater glory of God, and for a glossary of this code, call in Holmes).[1]

Why are Holmes and Watson called Cox and Box respectively in *FW*? The answer may be found in the first two introductory sentences to *The Problem of Thor Bridge*, which help to identify the *FW* personalities of the detective and his biographer in two or three passages and also seem to relate directly to the structure of the book itself.

"Somewhere in the vaults of Cox & Co. at Charing Cross, there is a travel-worn and battered tin dispatch-box with my name, John H. Watson, M.D., Late Indian Army, painted on the lid. It is crammed with papers nearly all of which are records of cases to illustrate the curious problems which Mr. Sherlock Holmes had at various times to examine."

We may assume that records of most of the published cases of Sherlock Holmes are in this box, although none are specifically named. By way of inventory, Watson mentions only three unpublished cases. In contrast to Watson's reticence, Joyce devotes almost three pages to a catalogue of names for the buried Mamafesta of Anna Livia Plurabelle. As Campbell and Robinson have pointed out, the Mamafesta "is the germ and substance of *Finnegans Wake* itself."[2] It is significant therefore that near the top of the second page of titles we find the following: (105.5–6) "*Through the Boxer-Coxer Rising in the House with the Golden Stairs.*"

Many readers may recognize Box and Cox as the name of a Victorian farce about two bachelors who share lodgings—like Watson and Holmes. However, neither the original comedy nor the later version set to music by Sir Arthur Sullivan has any relevance to a "*House with the Golden Stairs,*" which is plainly the bank of Cox & Co. From its underground vaults the Sherlockian canon has risen. Five other Mamafesta titles seem to have Sherlockian connotations:

(105.9–10) *"The Log of Anny to the Base All"(Black Peter)*

(105.28–29) *"How to Pull a Good Horus-Coup even when Oldsire is Dead to the World" (The Norwood Builder* and *Silver Blaze)*

(106.12–13) *"Siegfeld Follies and or a Gentlehomme's Faut Pas" (A Scandal in Bohemia)*

(106.14) *"A Pretty Brick Story for Childsize Heroes" (The Man with the Twisted Lip)*

(106.17–19) *"It Was Me Egged Him on to the Stork Exchange and Lent my Dutiful Face to His Customs" (The Stock-broker's Clerk)*

(371.2–5) "He did strongleholder ... sunkentrunk, that from tin of this clucken hadded runced slapottleslup. For him had hord from fard a piping."

Here we have suggestions of a vault (strongleholder), the tin box, the Inverness cloak and deerstalker (clucken hadded), the hoard of papers under the painted (fard) lid and Holmes's familiar tobacco pipe. But the pipe music heard from afar is the first verse of the "Ballad of the Sockerson Boy," which begins here. (371.6) Pages 370–71 include many allusions to the story of the resurrection of Sherlock Holmes in *The Adventure of the Empty House,* which will be discussed subsequently.

The association of Shem the Penman and Shaun the Post with the Mamafesta points to a similar relationship between Holmes and Watson in regard to the Sherlockian canon. The cases are the work of Holmes, but it is Watson who makes them known to the world. Sherlock Holmes is elsewhere identified with Shem. (180.5–6) "*Deal Lil Shemlockup Yellin*" is the title of a song sung by Shem himself. (228.15–16) "Shimach ... Mum's for's maxim, ban's for's book" combines Shem and Sherlock, both adopting the stratagem of "Silence, Exile and Cunning" from *A Portrait of the Artist as a Young Man.*[3]

In 1893 Arthur Conan Doyle grew so bored with writing Sherlock Holmes stories that he decided to kill off the great detective. Accordingly, he published *The Final Problem,* wherein Holmes supposedly died as the result of a great fall at the Reichenbach Falls in Switzerland. Fortunately, the corpse was never recovered, so Doyle was able to change his mind and bring Holmes back to life in *The Adventure of the Empty House* ten years later.

In experiencing death from a great fall, followed by the resurrection of his body, Sherlock Holmes reenacted more closely than any other character in modern literature the experience of the hero of an old Irish comic song, "Finnegan's Wake." Tim Finnegan, a hod carrier, fell from a high ladder one day and broke his skull. His widow laid out the corpse on the bed and called in his friends for a wake with the usual liquid refreshments. When the not-unusual fight broke out, a bottle of whiskey flew across the room, sprinkling Tim's body with the contents, whereupon the revivified Finnegan sat up in bed, shouting, "Souls to the Devil do you think I'm dead?"

James Joyce chose the name of the ballad for the name of his cryptic masterwork because his central theme is resurrection and reincarnation, eternally recurring human life and death. That Joyce omits the apostrophe makes the title a positive statement: *all* Finnegans wake. Eternal recurrence is emphasized in the very structure, which is circular. There is no beginning and no end; the final words of the last printed page are part of a sentence that begins the first printed page.

As "Mr. Sherlock Holmes Discourses" in *The Valley of Fear*: "Everything comes in circles, even Professor Moriarty. Jonathan Wild (ca. 1720) was the hidden force of the London criminals....The old wheel turns and the same spoke comes up. It's all been done before and will be again."

Joyce has tried to include in his Great Circle allusions to all the world's mythology, legendry and literature in one form or another. But because of its circular structure, narrated events do not occur in linear sequence. Furthermore, *FW* is a dream told in dream pictures. Names, faces, places and scenes rapidly appear, change, merge into each other, fade and reappear. To play all the parts in the complex "drame," Joyce has assembled a repertory company consisting of a Dublin pub keeper, HCE (Here Comes Everybody); his wife, ALP (Anna Livia Plurabelle); a daughter, Issy; quarreling twin sons, Shem the Penman and Shaun the Post; a housekeeper, Kate; and a mysterious manservant-bartender-policeman, named initially Sacksoun and subsequently many variations thereof. A large cast of supporting actors also appears as required.

Included in *FW* are allusions of varying clarity and significance to at least fifteen of the stories in the Holmesian canon. *The Sign of the Four* is structurally harmonious with *FW*, and references to this case are more frequent than to any other Sherlockian source. Among the supporting players in *FW* are Four Old Men who appear variously as the Four Evangelists, the Four Provinces of Ireland and other well known Fours, including the assignees of the Agra treasure. The Sholto twins make an appearance as Shem and Shaun, and the chart showing the hiding place for the Agra treasure has certain features in common with a mysterious letter from Boston, which is purported to provide a clue to understanding *FW* itself.

In addition to the Four Old Men there is another numbered group, the Twelve Morpios. They are identified variously as jurymen, Apostles of Christ and perhaps even the numbers on a clock. They are associated with words ending in the suffix "ation" and are almost certainly the twelve authors of the first-published, 1929 critical work on *FW*. Its title, suggested by Joyce himself, is *Our Exagmination round his Factification for Incamination of Work in Progress*.[4]

For Sherlockian purposes a more important individual is a countryman of Sigerson's, a Norwegian captain. When he is not trying to buy a new suit of clothes, he may be found in HCE's pub. Perhaps he is also known as Basil.

In the sixty pages of alphabetized literary allusions that form an appendix to his otherwise authoritative study, *The Books at the Wake*, James S. Atherton dismisses Sherlock Holmes with the notation that he is overtly named twice in *FW*. Conversely, he lists several possible references to the lesser works of Doyle, most notably as a source of information on spiritualism. Although the genius of Baker Street deserves greater recognition, it is entirely appropriate that the disguises assumed by the Master of the Art should have been more difficult to penetrate than those worn by mere amateurs. This special talent of the detective is apparent in one of Holmes's esoteric *FW* names, "Soteric Sulkinbored," and in his association with the shape-changing sea deity Proteus.

In *The Speckled Band* Holmes "chuckled heartily" when he was called a "Scotland Yard Jack-in-Office." For *FW* purposes, Joyce also confounds Holmes with the official detective force. As indicated above he is usually identified as a "comestabulish pollysigh" (German, *Polizei*). Holmes is made a symbol of British law, and therefore, by Joycean association, a symbol of British rule in Ireland. As a policeman he represents one of the two great forces of oppression in Victorian and Edwardian Ireland. Herbert Gorman quotes a

1904 entry in Joyce's notebook: "Spiritual and temporal power—Priests and police in Ireland."[5] The theme recurs in many forms throughout Joyce's work. That he thought it meet to set it down in his tables confirms its importance.

In including the Holmesian saga in the mythology of *FW*, Joyce has provided the publican of Chapelizod, Humphrey Chimpden Earwicker, with a familiar frame of reference. The criticism of Edmund Wilson that "instead of the myths growing out of Earwicker, Earwicker seems swamped in the myths,"[6] does not apply to the myth of Sherlock Holmes. Insofar as HCE may be the dreamer of *FW*, Holmes is a congruous dream figure.

(304 F3) "Wipe your glosses with what you know" has been interpreted as meaning that there is something in *FW* for every literate reader. Most assuredly what every reader knows is Sherlock Holmes. How is it then that this lowest common denominator, this somebody for everybody, should have remained unrecognized?

Perhaps the answer may be found in Joyce's apparent decree that that which is most familiar to the dreamer should be most heavily veiled to the reader. It is the commonplace that is often the most mysterious. The ordinary details of HCE's life are swamped in esoterica. The exact nature of his offense in the Phoenix Park is still uncertain. Giovanni Battista Vico is readily identified in *FW*. Sherlock Holmes is harder to find. To Joyce, the ordinary is the extraordinary.

The Italian philosopher Giovanni Battista Vico (1668–1724) is, in fact, the third person named in *FW* after Eve and Adam, on the second line of the book: (3.2) "Brings us by a commodius vicus of recirculation." The Vico Road describes a slight arc along the shore of Dublin Bay between Dalkey and Bray. But more to the point, "recirculation" refers to Vico's advocacy of the theory of the cyclical nature of human history which Joyce built into the structure of *FW*.

Another Italian philosopher important to *FW* is Giordano Bruno of Nola (1548-1600), who was burned at the stake as a heretic for preaching a pre-Hegelian doctrine of the unity of opposites. (92.8–11) "Equals of opposites ... polarized for reunion by the symphysis of their antipathies." Joyce alluded to this doctrine in association with the Sherlockian adventure of *The Man with the Twisted Lip*.

It should be emphasized that in most of the passages cited here, Sherlockian allusions are shared with those from other literary and historical sources. Indeed, in some cases the Sherlockian identification is obviously secondary. This study, therefore, does not necessarily conflict with any of the numerous scholarly interpretations of *FW* published over the years. Anna Livia Plurabelle has lost none of her other children. She has gained Sherlock Holmes.

NOTES

1. Both editions of *FW* are identically paginated and standardized at thirty-six lines to the full page. (New York: Viking Press, 1939. London: Faber and Faber, 1939).

2. Joseph Campbell and Henry Morton Robinson, *A Skeleton Key to Finnegans Wake* (New York: Viking Press, 1961), 18.

3. James Joyce, *A Portrait of the Artist as a Young Man* (New York: Compass, 1963), 247.

4. Richard Ellmann, *James Joyce* (New York: Oxford University Press, 1959), 626.

5. Herbert Gorman, *James Joyce* (New York: Farrar and Rhinehart, 1939), 135.

6. Edmund Wilson, "The Dream of H. C. Earwicker," in *The Wound and the Bow* (New York: Oxford University Press, 1965), 210.

(*FW* 25.5) Poppypap's a passport out.

"My decrepit Italian friend." From "The Adventure of the Final Problem" in *The Illustrated Sherlock Holmes Treasury* (New York: Avenel, 1976), 321.

Chapter 3

The Final Problem and The Empty House

Like Tim Finnegan, HCE, Finn MacCool and Humpty Dumpty, Sherlock Holmes had a great fall. It occurred at the Reichenbach Falls in Switzerland in 1891. Like Finn and Humpty Dumpty, the body of Holmes was scattered across the face of the earth from Tibet to Khartoum to Montpellier and points intermediate. But in the fourth year Holmes rose again from the dead and resumed his heroic career. Finn again.

We may begin our account of this event in Sherlock Holmes's career near the beginning of *The Final Problem,* wherein Holmes, his life threatened by Professor Moriarty, fled London for the Continent, disguised as an aged Italian priest. And by a happy chance we may begin Joyce's account of the same scene near the beginning of *FW*.

(25.5–6) "Poppypap's a passport out. And honey is the holiest thing ever was, hive, comb and earwax." The primary picture here is that of His Holiness the Pope, whose coat of arms bears crossed keys. The French word *passepartout* means "master key." Adherence to the teachings of the pope offers a passport out of this world through resurrection. But hiding behind the Holy Father is Sherlock Holmes, disguised as a humble, old Italian priest. The disguise provided a much-needed passport out of England to escape Moriarty's gang. Passepartout is also the name of the manservant in Jules Verne's novel *Around the World in Eighty Days*. This reminds us that Holmes also traveled part way around the world—as far as Tibet. Another connotation of passepartout may be the Baker Street Irregulars (they can go everywhere), with whom Holmes had a quasi-paternal relationship. Further, there may even be a hint of the detective's lineal descent from the Vernet family of French painters. "Art in the blood is liable to take the strangest forms." (It can develop in any direction — go anywhere.) Then we remember Holmes's one-time usage of morphine, an opium derivative, as a means of escape from the tedium of inactivity. Hence "Poppypap" suggests the opium poppy, *Papaver somniferum*. As for the association of Holmes with honey, that too has one aspect suggesting a resurrection. In *His Last Bow*, Holmes, after some years of quiescence raising bees in Sussex, returned to life as a British secret agent, revealing his identity by selling a German spy a copy of *Practical Handbook of Bee Culture* instead of British Naval signals.

If we seem to be reading too much of Sherlock Holmes in these two brief lines, let it be known that Joyce himself encouraged us to read as much as possible, depending on the extent of our information. (304 F3) "Wipe your glosses with what you know." What we know is Sherlock Holmes. And the "we" includes James Joyce, who knew more than the rest of us about almost everything else.

Page 517 of *FW* seems to be a transcription of an official interrogation at a coroner's inquest. Part of it describes the fatal event at the Reichenbach Falls. We shall try to interpret it a few lines at a time, necessarily leaving many words unexplicated.

(517.2–6) "Did one scrum then in the auradrama, the deff, after some clever play in the mud, mention to the other undesirable, a dumm, during diverse intentional instants, that upon the resume after the angerus, how for his deal he was a pigheaded Swede and to wend himself to a medicis?"

The scum and the undesirable are, respectively, Holmes, the deft one, and Watson, the dumb (stupid) one. As Holmes tells Watson later (auradrama—not witnessed by the auditor), he was very careful that the footprints at the scene confirmed the deception that he and Moriarty had perished together (clever play in the mud). The word "angerus" seems to combine "anger" and "Angelus"—the prayer said in commemoration of the Incarnation. In this case it is the incarnation of Holmes as a Norwegian named Sigerson (pigheaded Swede). Holmes would eventually wend his way back to Dr. Watson.

(517.7–9) "To be sore he did, the huggornut! Only it was turniphudded dunce, I beg your pardon, and he would jokes bowlderblow the betholder with his black masket off the bawling green."

Moriarty rushed at Holmes and "threw his long arms around me" (huggernut—like a juggernaut).34 The struggle was witnessed by Colonel Sebastian Moran. Holmes looked up and saw "a man's head against the darkening sky" (turniphudded). Moran tried to push boulders down on Holmes from above (bowlderblow).

(517.10) "Sublime was the warning!"

Moran's rocks may have been limestone. There is also a suggestion here that Holmes was "sublimated" in the chemical sense. His body disappeared, going from a solid to a gaseous state without passing through an intermediate liquid stage. Holmes did not fall into the water, and he later spent some months of his exile at a chemical laboratory in Montpellier conducting research.

(517.11) "The author, in fact, was mardred."

Holmes was the author of a deceptive letter to Watson in which he falsely claimed martyrdom. In fact, the other, Moriarty, was martyred, or murdered. "Moriarty"35 is a variation of the Irish clan name "Murtagh," hence "murdered" has an added meaning.

(517.12–16) "did he, the first spikesman, do anything to him, the last spokesman, when, after heaving some more smutt and chaff between them, they rolled together into the ditch together?"

"No, he had his teeth in the back of his head."

Moriarty fell a long time, "struck a rock, bounded off," possibly with his teeth pushed through his head.

(517.17–18) "Did Box then try to shine his puss?"

"No, but Cox did to shin the punman."

Did Watson try to disguise himself—as by blacking his face with shoe polish? No, but Holmes did assume a new identity in order to flee the gunman, Moran. Watson and Holmes are Box and Cox, of course, by reason of that precious box in the vault of Cox & Co. (Thor Bridge). Box and Cox are also Victorian farce characters who share lodgings, like Watson and Holmes.

(517.19–20) "The worsted crying that if never he looked on Leaverholma's again and the bester huing that he might ever save sunlife?"

Watson blamed himself for leaving Holmes alone, convinced that he would never see him again. Holmes ran away to save his life.

(517.21) "Trulytruly Asbestos he ever. And sowasso I never."

For the final words of *The Final Problem,* Watson borrowed the words of Plato mourning Socrates: "[Holmes] whom I shall ever regard as the best and wisest [sowasso] man whom I have ever known."[1]

(374.36–375.1) "How you fell from story to story like a sagasand to lie."

From *The Final Problem* to *The Empty House* the saga of Sigerson falling like a sack of sand was a lie. Sigerson shares this identification with two other Norwegians, Henrik Ibsen and his Masterbuilder, Halvard Solness, another hero who had a great fall. As a gesture of bravado, the Masterbuilder climbed to the tower of a newly built house and fell to his death.[2]

(228.13–14) "A conansdream of lodascircles, he here schlucefinis."

Conan plus conundrum equals "conansdream." Holmes traveled widely but returned (lodacircles); "schlucefinis" is an amalgam of the German *Schluss*, meaning "end," and "sluice." Addition of the redundant "finis" suggests that the complete word is a negated negation—the "end of an end," hence a resumption or resurrection following death in a waterfall. Conan's conundrum: When is a finish not a finish? When it's a schlucefinis!

(228.14–15) "Mischnary for the minestrary to all the sems of Aram."

After visiting the head lama in Tibet, Holmes "passed through Persia and paid a short but interesting visit to the Khalifa at Khartoum, the results of which I have communicated to the Foreign Office." Joyce's word "minestrary" combines "monastery," for the residence of the head lama, and "ministry" for the Foreign Office. The "sems of Aram" are the semitic Arabs.

(228.15–17) "Mum's for's maxim, ban's for's book and Dodgesome Dora for hedgehung sheolmastress." This sentence is generally recognized among Joyceans as a paraphrase of "silence, exile, and cunning," the maxim adopted by Stephen Dedalus when he resolved to leave Ireland and go to Paris in *A Portrait of the Artist as a Young Man*.[3] It also happens to be the identical strategy adopted by Sherlock Holmes when he fled from Moriarty. In the case of Stephen Dedalus we may take it as a self-dramatizing pose. For Holmes it was a question of life or death. "Dodgesome Dora"? Adaline Glasheen identifies her as DORA, the Defence of the Realm Act, in *A Second Census of Finnegans Wake*. This would not be incompatible with Sherlock Holmes, who was, after all, a defender of the realm. But Glasheen also names, but does not otherwise identify,

Dora Sigerson, a Dublin poetess.[4] If Stephen Dedalus took Dora Sigerson for a schoolmistress, it might suggest that Joyce recognized Holmes as the preceptor.

(228.29–34) "He would ... before of weighting midhook, by dear home trashold on the raging canal, for othersites of Jorden, (heave a hevy, waterboy!) ... fire off ... his farced epistol to the hibruws."

There are quick flickers of Sherlockian reference here. The farewell letter written by "dear Holmes" to "My dear Watson" was placed on a rock, weighted down by Holmes's cigarette case and marked with a hooked alpenstock (weighting midhook, by dear home). There is another allusion to Moran as a rock thrower (heave a hevy) and to the farewell letter as a hoax (farced epistle). The farced epistle to the high-brows is also read as an allusion to *Ulysses*—a playful bit of Joycean self-mockery.

(370.30–31) "Bounce! It is polisignstunter. The Sockerson boy. To pump the fire of the lewd into those soulths of bauchees."

Sherlock Holmes has bounced back!

(370.34–35) "Fyre maynoother endnow! Shatten up ship! Bouououmce! Nomo clandoilskins cheakinlevers!"

The Hon. Ronald Adair, second son of the earl of Maynooth, was murdered by Col. Sebastian Moran with an air gun because he discovered that Moran had been cheating at cards. Shut him up quick! Owe you, owe you, owe you! The word "cheakinlevers" suggests not only "leave us cheat" but also the lever of the air gun against Moran's cheek, and that Adair was chicken-livered in wanting to return the money won in partnership with Moran.

(371.16–17) "ere the sockson locked at the dure. Which he would, shuttinshure. And lave them to sture."

Holmes was on Moran's trail and would lock him in stir.

(371.25–28) "Tids, genmen, plays she been goin shoother off almaynoother onawares. ... Ashiffle ashuffle."

There is a hint here of gentlemen playing cards as well as a reference to the murder.

(363.8–9) "Deductive Almayne Rogers disguides his voice shetters behind hoax chestnote from exexive."

"Almayne" here is primarily "old man," since Holmes first appeared in the Adair case disguised as an bookseller. He addressed Watson in a "strange, croaking voice." The term "hoax chestnote" combines hoarse chest note with an allusion to the current hoax and also perhaps to the hoaxed farewell note, "exexive" is ex-ex-detective — a detective back at work.

(455.5–6) "It's the fulldress Toussaint's wakeswalk experdition after a bail motion from the chamber of horrus."

Note the references to resurrection (experdition) and to the famous wax bust (like Madame Tussaud's) of Sherlock Holmes which deceived Moran. The Egyptian god Horus, in order to escape the vengeance of his enemy, Set, lay in hiding for seventy-two days.

(57.20–25) "nevertheless Madam's Toshowus waxes largely more lifeliked. ... And there many have paused before that exposure of him by old Tom Quad, a flashback in which he sits sated, gowndabout."

The wax bust was "so admirably done that it was a perfect facsimile. It stood on a small pedestal table with an old dressing gown of Holmes's so draped around it that the illusion from the street was absolutely perfect."

(57.31–32) "Ceadurbar-atta-Cleath … the shadow of a huge outlander."

This is Moran who had served in the Indian Army (see a durbar). His first appearance in the empty house was as "the vague outline of a man a shade blacker than the blackness of the open door."

(58.9–24) "With … deprofound souspirs. Steady sullivans! Mannequins pause! Longtongs breach is fallen down … fire firstshot, Missiers the Refuseleers! Peingpeong!"

Col. Moran opened and closed the breech of his air gun and took aim, giving "a little sigh of satisfaction" (French *soupir*, sigh). Mrs. Hudson, Holmes's housekeeper, was not moving the wax dummy at the moment (Mannequins pause). "There was a strange, loud whiz and a long silvery tinkle of broken glass" (Peingpeong).

(79.31–35) "and beggars bullets, if not worse, sending salmofarious germs in gleefully through the smithereen panes—Widow Strong, then, as her weaker had turned him to the wall (Tiptiptip!), did most all the scavenging from Good King Hamlaugh's gulden dayne."

Mrs. Hudson, sometimes called Kate, here called "Widow Strong," had been in the sitting room, below the level of the window, turning the wax dummy from time to time.

(113.21–22) "Kate takes charge of the waxworks."

"I'm afraid it [Moran's bullet] has spoilt your beautiful bust, for it passed right through the head and flattened itself on the wall. I picked it up from the carpet [did most all the scavenging]. Here it is!"

(276.F2) "For jolly comes smashing Holmes."

The official interrogation, previously noted, now turns its attention to Moran's air gun.

(518.15–18) "The illegallooking range or fender, alias turfing iron ... changed feet several times as briers revulvered42 during the weaponswap? Piff?"

"Puff, Excuse yourself, it was an ersatz lottheringcan."

Compressed air is suggested by "Piff ... Puff ... lottheringcan." We also see range finder and valve as well as "made in Germany"—"ersatz."

"Holmes had picked up the powerful air gun from the floor, and was examining its mechanism...."I knew Von Herder, the blind German mechanic, who constructed it."

(517.22) "That forte carlysle touch breaking the campdens pianoback."

Thomas Carlyle not only wrote *Sartor Resartus*, with its very strong relevance to the art of disguise,[5] but also a political essay entitled *Shooting Niagara*. Used as a noun, the Italian word *piano* means "plan." The name of the *Empty House* was Camden House. The sentence tells us that Holmes's stratagems spoiled the assassination plan of Camden House.

NOTES

1. Plato, *Phaido,* Translation Benjamin Jowett. The concluding paragraph: "Such was the end, Echecrates, of our friend [Socrates]; concerning whom I may truly say, that of all the men of his time whom I have known, he was the wisest and justest and best."

2. "When Joyce first began to nurse ambitions of becoming an author, Ibsen was the writer whom he chose as a model....The play that seems to be used most [in *FW*] is *The Masterbuilder*....Dozens of other examples could be given from every other part of the *Wake*." James S. Atherton, *The Books at the Wake* (New York: Viking Press, 1960), 152–157.

3. James Joyce, *A Portrait of the Artist as a Young Man* (New York: Compass, 1963), 247.

4. Adaline Glasheen, *A Second Census of Finnegans Wake* (Evanston, Ill.: Northwestern University Press, 1963) 66, 239.

5. *Sartor Resartus* by Thomas Carlyle purports to be an exposition for English readers of the life and thoughts of a great German philosopher, Diogenes Teufelsdrockh, author of *Clothes, Their Origin and Influence.* The central tenet of Clothes Philosophy is that man, by nature a naked animal, "by purpose and device masks himself in Clothes." Sherlock Holmes clearly understood this philosophy, for he made its practice part of his life's work: synthetically when he disguised himself; analytically when he penetrated the disguises of others. In Teufelsdrockh (Devil's Dung) Carlyle created a personality with many amusing eccentricities. Conan Doyle, who greatly admired Carlyle, borrowed many of these eccentricities for the personality of Holmes. As will be observed, Teufelsdrockh is directly identified with Holmes in two cases noted in FW.

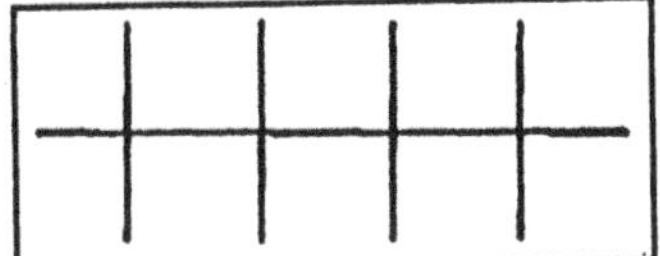

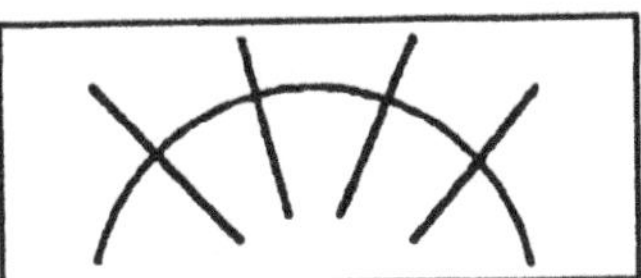

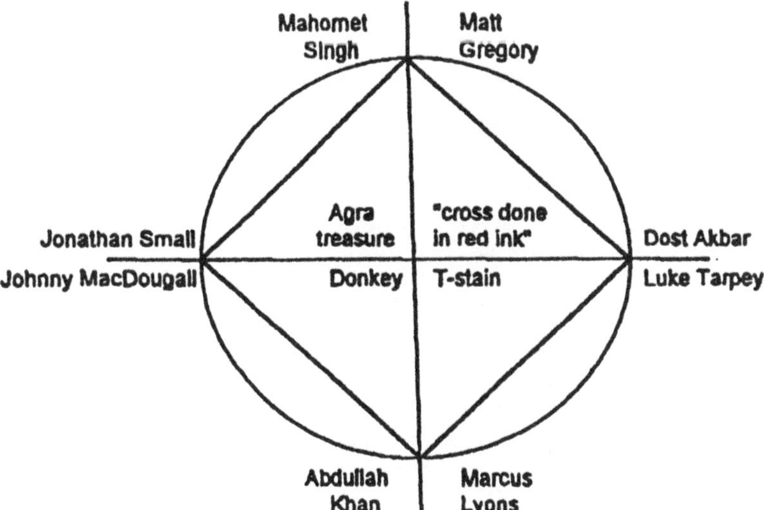

(*The Sign of the Four*) a curious hieroglyphic like four crosses in a line with their arms touching.

(*FW* 111.16–17) must now close it with the fondest to the twoinns with four crosskisses. . . .

Quincunx and Mandala symbols derived from *The Sign of the Four* (after Clive Hart). Drawn by William D. Jenkins.

Chapter 4

The Sign of the Four

"Sherlock Holmes took his bottle from the corner of the mantelpiece, and his hypodermic syringe from its neat morocco case. With his long, white, nervous fingers he adjusted the delicate needle and rolled back his left shirtcuff. For some little time his eyes rested thoughtfully upon the sinewy forearm and wrist, all dotted and scarred with innumerable puncture marks."

The first paragraph of the second published Sherlock Holmes story depicts the great detective as a quondam cocaine addict. The scene seems to be reflected in what may be the first *FW* allusion to Sherlock Holmes. (5.5–7) "Of the first was he to bare arms and a name: Wassaily Booseleaugh of Riesengeborg. His crest of huroldry, in vert with ancillars, troublant, argent, a hegoak, poursuivant."

"Wassaily" (Vasily) is Russian for "Basil." A possible identification is with "Captain Basil," an alias used by Holmes in *The Adventure of Black Peter*. "Riesengeborg" is identified with Reichenbach. In the *Encyclopaedia Britannica* (11th edition), the first entry for Reichenbach is "a town … at the foot of the Eulenbirge, a spur of the Reisengebirge." As for "ancillars, troublant, argent, a hegoak, poursuivant," every word could be applied very appropriately to Holmes' ancillary detective police force, the Baker Street Irregulars. They appear in *The Sign of the Four* as a squad of pursuing urchins (hedgehogs—hegoak poursuivant) whose wage was a silver (argent) shilling each.

Watson would soon cure Holmes of the cocaine habit, to which Holmes resorted out of sheer boredom. " 'My mind,' he said, 'rebels at stagnation. Give me problems, give me work, give the most abstruse cryptogram, or the most intricate analysis, and I am in my own proper atmosphere. I can dispense then with artificial stimulants.' "

This self-portrait of Sherlock Holmes, sulky and bored with inaction, yearning for salvation in an "abstruse cryptogram" is included in a passage of seven lines wherein we find, in sequence, allusions to the title of the story, the author's name, the hero, the murder victim and a plot detail. (393.2–8) "signs on the salt ... And still and all at that time of the dynast days of old konning Soteric Sulkinbored and Bargomaster Bart, when they struck coil."

In *The Sign of the Four*, Abdullah Khan, a Sikh, declares that the Agra treasure is " 'the due of those who have been true to their salt' " (signs on the salt). Doyle is "konning" and "Soteric Sulkinbored" is Sherlock Holmes. "Bargomaster Bart" is Bartholomew Sholto, the murder victim. He is identified with Ibsen's *Masterbuilder* (*Bygmester* in Norwegian) because Sholto climbed to the top of his house to find the Agra treasure hidden in a garret. At the scene of the murder there is both a coil of pipe and a puddle of oily creosote (struck coil). Perhaps "dynast" includes a reference to the murder (die nasty).

A great many allusions to *The Sign of the Four* occur in the "Mamalujo" chapter, devoted to Matthew, Mark, Luke and John. "Mamalujo" (383–399) is one of the shortest chapters in *FW* and the one that Joyce completed first. It seems further distinguished by a special quality of integrity. It is the story of Tristan and Isolde, and the somewhat mawkish love story of Watson and Mary Morstan in the context of *FW*.

Let us consider how the names of the Four Old Men in *FW*, Matt Gregory, Marcus Lyons, Luke Tarpey and Johnny MacDougall, relate to the Four in Doyle's story, Mahomet Singh, Abdullah Khan, Dost Akbar and Jonathan Small. Adaline Glasheen has remarked that Johnny MacDougall is "somehow most important of the Four. He is always a little separate from the other three."[1] The explanation for this distinction may be found in *The Sign of the Four*. Jonathan Small is the only active representative of his Four. As for the other three, (397.23–4) "it so happen they were all sycamore and by the world forgot." They were Sikhs, blackamoors, sentenced to life imprisonment in the Andaman Islands. Also (384.1–4) "the sycamores and the wild geese ... all four of them." Indian soldiers in British service are compared to "Wild Geese," historically Irish soldiers in French service. Incidentally, the names of Doyles three "Sikhs" are more like those of Muslims.

1. Matt Gregory: Glasheen is right in speculating on an association with Lady Augusta Gregory.[2] The Sikh half of Mahomet Singh's name is also Synge. (392.14–20) "And where do you leave Matt Emeritus? The laycheif of Abbottabishop? And exchullard or ffrench and gherman. Acoch! They were all so sorgy for poorboire Matt in his saltwater hat, with the Aran crown ... poor Matt, the old perigrime matriarch."

Mahomet Singh was dishonorably discharged from the Indian Army (Latin *emeritus*, retired soldier.) But Matt Gregory is also J. M. Synge, codirector of the Abbey Theatre (Abbotabishop) along with Yeats and Lady Gregory (matriarch), ex-scholar in France and Germany, and author of *The Aran Islands* and *Riders to the Sea*, with its sorrow and soggy (sorgy) drownings.

(387.29–32) "he was completely drowned off Erin's Isles ... and thank God, as Saman said, there were no more of him." From *Riders to the Sea*: "MAURYA....They're all gone now, and there isn't anything more the sea can do to me ... I'll have no call now to be going down and getting Holy Water in the dark nights after Samhain." Samhain (Saman) is the ancient Celtic Halloween.

(482.22–28) "Sometimes he would keep silent a few minutes as if in prayer ... he would not mind anybody who would be talking to him or crying stinking fish. ... Your too farfar a cock of the north there, Matty Armagh, and your due south so." Atherton has identified this passage as a parody of the speech that follows the one above.[3] "MAURYA ... if its only a bit of wet flour we do have to eat, and maybe a fish that would be stinking. (She kneels down again, crossing herself, and saying prayers under her breath.)"

2. Marcus Lyons: His name derives primarily from the heraldic symbol, the winged Lion of St. Mark. But his personality is strongly that of Marco Polo the Venetian, who won the nickname "Marco Millioni" for his million lies (Marco's Lyings). Thus he may be remotely associated with Doyle's Abdullah Khan by way of Kubla Khan. Marco Polo is a Tristan figure because he brought the Princess Kukachin from the court of Kubla Khan by sea to Persia so that she might marry the khan of that country.

(489.29–33) "South I see. You're up-in-Leal-Ulster and I'm free-Down-in-Easia. ... The prouts who will invent a writing there ultimately is the poeta, still more learned, who discovered the raiding there originally." The South of Ireland identifies Marcus Lyons and Asia identifies Marco Polo, who is sometimes credited with introducing block printing to Europe from China; "prouts" may combine Gutenberg (krauts) with Father Prout, the versifier and Proust.

(387.36–388.3) "The new world presses. Where the old conk cruised now croons the yunk. Exeunc throw a darras Kram of Llawnroc, ye gink guy, kirked into yourd. Enterest atawonder Wehpen, luftcat revol, fairescapading in his natsirt." The "old conk" is the Great Khan and conqueror, and probably also Conchubor, the King Mark type in Synge's *Deidre of the Sorrows*. Marco Polo traveled with his uncle. There is a reference to a printing press followed by an interesting device. "Mark of Cornwall ... king ... nephew, tactful lover ... Tristan" is printed backward — right to left in the Chinese manner. (Cf. *U* 122: "He stayed in his walk to watch a typesetter neatly distributing type. Reads it backwards first. Quickly he does it. Must require some practice that. mangiD kcirtaP.") Marco Polo's interest in the wonder weapon, gunpowder, is also noted, as is the gingko tree (gink guy), another European import from China.

3. Luke Tarpey: He is identified with the Sikh, Akbar, and his surname is derived from Tarpeia, a Roman girl who betrayed the citadel to the Sabines, bribed with the promise of jewelry. Similarly Dost Akbar brought the merchant Achmet into the guarded fort at Agra, where Achmet was murdered for the sake of the treasure. From *The Sign of the Four*:

"Achmet is now in the city of Agra and desires to gain his way into the fort.... Dost Akbar has promised this night to lead him to a side-postern of the fort." (386.6–10) "Luke and Johnny MacDougall and all wishening for anything at all of the bygone times ... for four farback tumblefuls of woman squash." Tarpeia was crushed to death by the shields of the Sabines (woman squash) and thrown from the summit of the Tarpeian rock (tumblefuls). (390.32–33) "Woman. Squash. Part. Ay, ay." An anagram for "Tarpeia" is apparent here.

4. Johnny MacDougall: The name "MacDougall" is derived from the same Gaelic root as "Dublin." The meaning is "dark water." Jonathan Small lost his leg in the Ganges and his treasure in the Thames. He was captured when his wooden leg sank deep in the black mud of the Thames bankside.

In the "Mamalujo" chapter Sherlock Holmes is usually called "Lally" rather than any of the Sigerson cognates. A possible reason is that Joyce completed "Mamalujo" before the other chapters, and perhaps he had not yet worked out the Sigerson identity. However, Lally does appear early in Book I as a policeman. (67.10–11) "Long Lally Tobkids, the special, sporting a fine breast of medals." In *The Sign of the Four* the Sholto family at different times had two Indian servants named Lal-Lal Chowdar and Lal Rao. Thus in *FW* Holmes appears sometimes as a policeman and sometimes as a servant, like Sockerson, Sickerson and so on.

(387.19–20) "Fair Margrate waited Swede Villem and Lally in the rain." Mary Morstan, Watson and Holmes waited in the rain to be conducted to the house of Thaddeus Sholto. Thaddeus and Bartholomew were twins, and there was conflict between them—a Shem-Shaun relationship.

(390.1–10) "forget the past, when the burglar he shoved the wretch in the churneroil, and contradicting all about Lally ... in the Locklane Lighthouse earing his wick with a pierce of railing and liggen hig with his ladder up, and ... the old croniony Skelly, with the lether belly, full of neltts, full of keltts, full of lightweight beltts and all the bald drakes or ever he had up in the bohereen, off Artsichekes Road, with Moels and Mahmullagh Mullarty, the man in the Oran mosque."

This passage is a conflation of both Sholto twins and both their houses; they did not live together. Thaddeus Sholto's house, in Coldharbour Lane, was "dark save for a single glimmer in the kitchen window" (in the Locklane Lighthouse). Thaddeus described his house as "an oasis of art in the howling desert of South London." He is thus an "artsy sheikh" (Artsichekes). "Moels" is Welsh for "bald" and for "mountain." Thaddeus Sholto had "a very high head, a bristle of red hair all around the fringe of it, and a bald, shining scalp which shot out from among it like a mountain peak." Thaddeus was eager to "forget the past" and to share the treasure with Mary Morstan. He told the story of his father's death, how a burglar had broken in and searched the cupboards and boxes.

The house of Bartholomew Sholto, Pondicherry Lodge, Norwood, was guarded by an Irish prize-fighter named McMurdo, who happened to be an old sparring partner of Sherlock Holmes (the old croniony Skelly, with the lether belly, full of keltts, full of lightweight beltts). The treasure seekers had left the grounds of Pondicherry Lodge pitted and cluttered with mounds of dirt "as though all the moles in England had been let loose in it" (Moels). Bartholomew had locked himself in his room and would not answer (liggen hig with his ladder up). He was found murdered with a poisoned thorn "stuck in the skin just above the ear" (earing his wick with a pierce of railing). In one corner of the room a wicker-covered carboy of creosote trickled a stream of dark liquid (the wretch in the churneroil).

(388.24–27) "in single combat, under the sycamores . . . behind the century man on the door." Another recollection of the boxing match between Holmes and the sentry, McMurdo.

The scene of the *FW* chapter immediately preceding "Mamalujo" is set in HCE's pub. Throughout the chapter the many customers at the bar converse, while a television set adds other voices and other pictures. Appearing on television are the warring twins, Shem and Shaun. In this chapter they are called Butt and Taff (Bart and Tad—Bartholomew and Thaddeus Sholto). Perhaps the TV set is not working well (after all, this was pre-1939), because at one point, Butt and Taff merge on the screen, apparently switch identities and separate again. (349.7–9) "(*In the heliotropical noughttime following a fade of transformed Tuff and, pending its viseversion, a metenergic reglow of beaming Batt*)." The passage recalls Watson's first sight, through a keyhole, of the murdered Bartholomew in *The Sign of the Four*: "Moonlight was streaming into the room and it was bright with a vague and shifty radiance. Looking straight at me, and suspended, as it were, in the air, for all beneath was in shadow, there hung a face—the very face of our companion, Thaddeus. ... So like was the face to that of our little friend that I looked round at him to make sure that he was indeed with us."

(350.11–12) "BUTT (*with a gisture expansive of Mr. Lhugewhite Cadderpollard with sunflowered beauton hole*)." A term of disgust applied to Oscar Wilde was "Great White Caterpillar." But also included is the "large blue" (Lhuge) Caterpillar who smokes a hookah in *Alice in Wonderland*. That these two are now identified with Bart confirms the switch of roles, for Bart was the hard-headed, acquisitive brother, while Tad was the effeminate aesthete who smoked the hookah. Atherton observes: "This idea of a change of personality in a dream is first mentioned in *Alice in Wonderland* when Alice meets the Caterpillar: ' "Who are *you*?" said the Caterpillar. Alice replied, rather shyly, "I—I hardly know, Sir, just at present—at least I know who I *was* when I got up this morning, but I think I must have changed several times since then." ' "[4]

The Sholto twins quarreled over the disposition of the Agra treasure, inherited from their father. Bartholomew was murdered and Thaddeus was arrested for the crime, but he was cleared by Sherlock Holmes. The first Sherlockian allusions occur at the very opening of the television broadcast.

(338.5–9) "TAFF (*a smart boy, of the peat freers, thirty two eleven, looking through the roof towards a ... solation to the rhyttel in his hedd*) ... blurty moriartsky blutcherudd?" Thaddeus is a small man whose bald dome emerges from a fringe of hair like "like a mountain peak from fir trees" (peat freers?). He has "just turned his thirtieth year" (thirty two eleven). The "rhyttel in his hedd" concerns the riddled head of his sole relation (solation), Bartholomew, who was "blutcherudd" by a dart from a blowgun "just above the ear." The murderer (in this case *not* Professor "moriartsky") entered "looking through the roof."

(338.11–13) "BUTT (*mottledged youth, clergical appealance, who, as his pied friar, is supposing to motto the sorry de jester in tifftaff toffiness or to be disgarced from ever and a daye in his accounts*)." In his argument with Bart, Tad took a gentlemanly position and quoted a "toffy" French motto: "It would have been such bad taste to have treated a young lady in so scurvy a doctor. '*Le mauvais goût mène au crime.*' The French have a very neat way of putting these things." The French words *geste* and *dégoûter* appear in "de jester." As a dead man, Bart had a "clergical appealance."

(340.11–14) "TAFF (*a blackseer, he stroves to regulect all the straggles for wife in the rut of the past through the widnows in effigies keening after the blank sheets in their faminy ...*). Oh day of rath! Ah, murther of mines!" Tad recollects the story of his father's death. The face of a vengeful enemy peered through the windows at the deathbed scene.

(345.4–7) "TAFF (*as a marrer of act, prepensing how such, waldmanns from Burnias seduced country clowns ... after to see him pluggy well moidered as a murder effect, you bet your blowie knife*)." The murderer of Bart, Tonga, and an Andaman Island dwarf made a living in England by putting on a Wild Man from Borneo act "at fairs and other such places as the black cannibal. He would eat and dance his war dance," as Jonathan Small narrated. Small had hoped to return from India with his "pockets full of gold moidores" (moidered).

(345.12–15) "BUTT (*goes on kuldrum like without asking for prepeace or anysing a soul*). Merzmard! I met with whom it was too late. My fate! O hate! … And think of that when you smugs to bagot." The passage suggests that *The Sign of the Four* resembles Wagner's *Ring of the Nibelungs* (without … anysing). Bart goes on like Gutrune (kuldrum like). The Agra treasure was lost in the Thames, as the Rhine gold was returned to the Rhine maidens (Merzmard). And think of that when you gloat over the baguette and other jewels (smugs to bagot).

(346.15–19) "TAFF (*now as he has been past the buckthurnsttock from Peadhur Piper … and find your pollyvouley foncey pitchin ingles in the parler*)….The fourscore soculums are watchyoumaycodding to cool the skoopgoods bloof … tway fainmain stod op to slog, free bond men lay lurking on." The dart from Tonga's blowpipe was a black thorn stuck in the skin. There is another allusion to Tad's fancy French epigram (pollyvoulley foncey). The Four were played for suckers (soculums) and they wanted to even the score. The senior Sholto scooped up the treasure (skoopgoods) and there was a blow-off (bloof). Two men (tway fainmen) left the Andaman Islands, three were still there as prisoners (free bond men).

(347.26–348.1) "TAFF (*smolking his fulverite turfkish in the rooking pessence of laddios*)." Tad smoked his Turkish water pipe in a lady's presence. " 'Miss Morstan? … I trust that you have no objection to tobacco smoke, to the balsamic odour of the Eastern tobacco. I am a little nervous and I find my hookah an invaluable sedative.' "

(165.30–36) "The boxes, if I may break the subject gently, are worth about fourpence pourbox but I am inventing a more patent process, foolproof and pryperfect (I should like to ask that Shedlock Holmes person who is out for removing the roofs of our criminal classics by what *deductio ad domumun* he hopes *de tacto* to detect anything unless he happens of himself *movibile tectu* to have a slade off)."

This passage alludes not only to Doyle and Oscar Slater, but also most clearly to *The Sign of the Four* and the theft of the box with the Agra treasure. First there is the idea of breaking open the box, which is worth fourpence. The dwarf, Tonga, entered the Sholto home illegally (Shedlock Homes) by means of the roof (*movibile tectu* — Latin *tectum,* roof) and displaced some of the slates. Holmes himself climbed through the trap door to the roof and observed, " 'Tiles were loosened the whole way along.' "

(394.18) "Lally of the cleftoff bagoderts and Roe of the fair cheats." Holmes found the bag of darts left at the crime scene by Tonga. "Roe of the fair cheats" are the offspring of Morstan and Sholto.

(389.6–7) "Killorcure and Killthemall and Killeachother and Killkelly on the Flure." This expresses the philosophy of Tonga—"the little bloodthirsty imp," as Small describes him.

(392.29–30) "gripping an old pair of curling tongs ... to blow his brains with." Again, Tonga with his blowgun.

(392.36–393.2) "and all on account of ... Shakeltin and stratchman and his mouth watering, acid and alkolic; signs on the salt." Holmes employed a dog (scratchman) to sniff out the trail of the criminals from the creosote puddle. Besides creosote the laboratory of the murder victim contained carboys of various chemicals.

The most intriguing use by James Joyce of a Sherlock Holmes story occurs in the chapter concerning the "Mamafesta" letter from Boston (104–25).

(111.9–20) "a goodish-sized sheet of letterpaper originating by transhipt from Boston (Mass.) of the last of the first ... & allathome's ... must now close it with fondest to the twoinns with four crosskisses for holy paul holey corner holipoli whollyisland pee ess from (locust may eat all but this sign shall they never)....The stain, and that a teastain."

This passage is part of the description of ALP's Mamafesta. It is also part of the description of the chart showing the original hiding place of the Agra treasure. Holmes commented: " 'It is a paper of native Indian manufacture....At one point is a small cross done in red ink....In the left-hand corner is a curious hieroglyphic like four crosses in a line with their arms touching. Beside it is written in very rough and coarse characters, "The sign of the four — Jonathan Small, Mahomet Singh, Abdullah Khan, Dost Akbar." ' "

It will be noted that the *FW* passage alludes to the Sholto twins. As regards the treasure, these two were in (twoinns), the others were out. The single small cross marking the treasure appears in "locust" (locus), but more importantly in "teastain" (T-stain, tau cross and perhaps TrEAsure). And of course, tea is thrown into water as the Agra treasure was thrown into the Thames.

A comparison of "letterpaper originating by transhipt from Boston (Mass.) of the last of the first" with Holmes's "paper of native Indian manufacture" reveals a most interesting subtlety: an allusion to the Boston Tea Party with the East Indians becoming American Indians (Cooper's *Last of the Mohicans*—the last of the first Americans). That the tea was thrown into Boston Harbor provides another correspondence with the Agra treasure.

As for *FW*'s "four crosskisses" and Holmes's "four crosses in a line with their arms touching," Clive Hart has observed with strong relevance, "One of the most obvious symbolic crosses in *Finnegans Wake* is that which Joyce assigns to the Four Old Men *FW*: (119.28). This, a quincunx, is defined by five points (as its name implies), the fifth of which — the central point represents the Donkey on whom they all four ride *FW*: (557.2). The Donkey is the 'carryfour' ... or the crossroads on which they all converge *FW*: (581.22)."[5]

Inasmuch as the fifth cross on the Agra treasure map represents the treasure itself, the central point of existence for the four men of the Sign, we must add still another complexity to the already overloaded Donkey symbolism in *FW*. There are several observations consistent with a Donkey-Agra treasure identification. Hart refers to the "constantly frustrated strivings of the Four to reach the center of the cross."[6] Adaline Glasheen states that the Four conduct a coroner's inquest over a treasure trove. "As for treasure-troves, the Four are entirely taken up with one from 477.35–501.5"[7]

In *Julius Caesar* IV, i, Antony offers a classical donkey-treasure nexus:

> This is a slight, unmeritable man,
> Meet to be sent on errands; ...
> And though we lay these honours on this man ...
> He shall but bear them as the ass bears gold, ...

> And having brought our treasure where we will,
> Then take we down his load, and turn him off,
> Like to the empty ass, to shake his ears
> And graze in commons.

(483.16–18) "I'll see you moved farther blarneying Marcantonio! What cans such wretch to say to I or how have My to doom with him?" That the attitude of Antony and Octavius to Lepidus exactly reflects that of Morstan and Sholto to the Four is striking.

The discussion of the letter continues: (119.27–32) "a multiplication marking for crossroads ahead, which you like pothook for the family gibbet, their old fourwheedler for the bucker's field, a teat anyway for a tryst someday, and his onesidemissing for an allblind alley leading to an Irish plot in the Champ de Mors, not?"

A betrayal or double cross is suggested by "crossroads ahead" and by "Irish plot." The agreement over the treasure was a sacrament in which they all partook (pothook). They would all meet (tryst) someday and share the treasure. Jonathan Small's missing leg is apparent in "onesidemissing," and "Mors, not" is an anagram for Morston.

(124.1–35) "it was but pierced butnot punctured.... These paper wounds, four in type ... and following up their one true clue, the circumflexuous wall of a singleminded men's asylum.... Yard inquiries pointed out → that they ad bîn 'provoked' ay ^ fork, of à grave Brofèsor; àth é's Brèak—fast—table; ... Small need after that."

The four holes in ALP's letter are matched by holes in the Agra treasure chart, one at each corner: (111.18) "holey corner." Holmes noted that the map " 'has at some time been pinned to a board. The diagram upon it appears to be a plan of part of a large building with numerous halls, corridors and passages."

The diagram is that of the old Agra fort. The phrase "singleminded men's asylum" suggests both the fort and the Andaman Islands penal colony. The "Yard" is of course Scotland Yard, and the symbol Æ suggests Tonga's poisoned dart—with which Bartholomew Sholto had been most "professionally piqued." We also see an allusion to Oliver Wendell Holmes, *The Professor at the Breakfast Table*, who was Sherlock Holmes's godfather. Finally, Jonathan Small's need of the treasure is noted.

(389.34–390.1) "Lally when he lost part of his half a hat and all belongings to him in his old futile manner, cape, towel and drawbreeches and repeating himself and telling him now for the seek of Senders Newslaters."

First there is the strange image, "half a hat," which recurs in this chapter. In the case of Lally, perhaps it means Holmes's deerstalker cap, which has a brim in front and back but no brim on the sides.[8] The loss of clothing means a change of identity. Holmes had returned to Baker Street disguised as "a respectable master mariner," wearing a single-peaked seaman's cap (lost part of his half a hat). He decided to play a joke on Watson and Athelney Jones, the Scotland Yard man, who were waiting for him. The seaman would not state his business to Watson and Jones, but insisted on speaking to Holmes and to Holmes only (repeating himself). He was therefore obliged to await Holmes's return (for the seek of Senders Newslaters). When Holmes removed his disguise, Athelney Jones, the Welshman, was "highly delighted" at the joke. (390.12–14) "and he couldn't stop laughing over Tom Tip Tarpey, the Welshman, and the four middle-aged widowers."

(263, left margin)

"Mars speaking."
"Smith, no home."
"Non quod sed quiat."
"Hearasay in paradox lust."

Sherlock Holmes traced Small and Tonga to a Thames boatyard, where the criminals had hired a steam launch for the getaway. The boatman's name was Mordecai
Smith. Holmes began a conversation with Mrs. Smith by complimenting her on her son:

" 'A fine child, Mrs. Smith.'

" 'Lor' bless you, sir, he is that, and forward. He gets a'most too much for me to manage, 'specially when my man is away days at a time' (*Ma's speaking*).

" 'Away, is he?' said Holmes in a disappointed voice. 'I am sorry for that, for I wanted to speak to Mr. Smith' " (*Smith, no home*).

Holmes pretended that he wanted to hire Smith's steam launch. In the course of the conversation he obtained a description of the boat.

" 'Ah! She's not that old green launch with a yellow line, very broad in the beam?'

" 'No, indeed. She's as trim a little thing as any on the river. She's been freshly painted, black with two red streaks' " (*Non quod sed quiat*—not that, because).

After the interview Holmes comments to Watson on his technique: " 'The main thing with people of that sort ... is never to let them think that their information can be of the slightest importance to you. If you do, they will instantly shut up like an oyster. If you listen to them under protest, as it were, you are very likely to get what you want' " (*Hearasay in paradox lust*).

(373.9–11) "The gangstairs strain and anger's up as Hosty rares the can and cup To speed the bogre's barque away O'er wather parted from the say."

Holmes proposed, " 'One bumper ... to the success of our little expedition' " before boarding the police launch for the angry pursuit of the gangsters down the Thames.

(391.18–35) "made a Neptune's mess of all of himself, sculling over the giamonds courseway, and because he forgot to remember to sign an old morning proxy paper ... poor Dion Cassius Poosycomb, all drowned too ... (well he was shocking poor in his health, he said, with the shingles falling off him) ... so sorry he was, really, because he left the bootybutton in the handsome cab."

During the chase down the Thames, Small scattered the Agra treasure in the river, "rather than let it go to kith or kin of Sholto or Morstan." Tonga, who "could climb like a cat" (Poosycomb—knocked the shingles off the roof) was shot and fell overboard. Subsequently Watson left a police inspector waiting in a cab while he took the empty treasure chest in to Mary Morstan's house. "A very patient man was that inspector in the cab."

(387.29–32) "He was completely drowned off Erin's Isles at that time ... and thank God, as Saman said there were no more of him." Both Tonga and the treasure were lost in the Thames. The treasure no longer an impediment, Watson was now free to marry Mary Morstan. " 'Thank God!' I [Watson] ejaculated from my very heart."

(398.11–12) "Now let us ran on to say oremus prayer and homey sweet homely."

NOTES

1. Adaline Glasheen, *A Second Census of Finnegans Wake* (Evanston, Ill.: Northwestern University Press, 1963), 159.

2. Ibid., 100.

3. James S. Atherton, *The Books at the Wake* (New York: Viking Press, 1960), 284.

4. Ibid., 128.

5. Clive Hart, *Structure and Motif in Finnegans Wake* (Evanston, Ill.: Northwestern University Press, 1962), 135.

6. Ibid., 136.

7. Glasheen, *Second Census*, 1i.

8. *Finnegans Wake* is (20.16) "Doublends Jined." Like Sherlock Holmes's half a hat, it begins and ends the same way. Stephen Dedalus (*U* 17) wears a "Latin Quarter hat" and Leopold Bloom (*U* 56) wears two thirds of a hat: "Plasto's high grade ha" (sic).

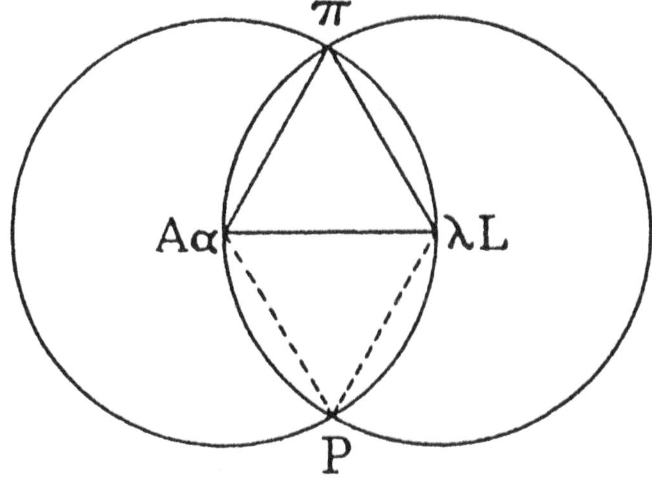

Buried treasures are naturally among the problems which have come to Mr. Holmes. One genuine case was accompanied by a diagram here reproduced. It refers to an Indiaman which was wrecked upon the South African coast in the year 1782. . . .

The ship contained a remarkable treasure, including, I believe, the old crown regalia of Delhi. It is surmised that they buried these near the coast, and that this chart is a note of the spot. Each Indiaman in those days had its own semaphore code, and it is conjectured that the three marks upon the left are signals from a three-armed semaphore. Some record of their meaning might perhaps even now be found in the old papers of the India Office. The circle upon the right gives the compass bearings. The larger semi-circle may be the curved edge of a reef or of a rock. The figures above are the indications of how to reach the X which marks the treasure. Possibly they may give the bearings as 186 feet from the 4 upon the semi-circle.

From *Memories and Adventures: The Autobiography of Sir Arthur Conan Doyle* (Boston: Little, Brown, 1923), 109–10.

Chapter 5

The Dancing Men and The Valley of Fear

The clearest *FW* passage identifying Sherlock Holmes as an expert cryptographer is associated with the *The Sign of the Four:* (530.17–22) "Where's that gendarm auxiliar, arianautic sappertillery, that reported on the whole hoodlum, relying on his morse-erse wordybook and the trunchein up his tail? Roof Seckesign van der Deckel and get her story from him! Recall Sickerson, the lizzyboy! Seckerson magnon of Errick. Sackerson! Hookup!"[1]

The coroner's inquest which investigated the incident at Reichenbach is still in session. Now the inquiry is concerned with the Mamafesta, the letter from Boston, and Holmes is called as an expert witness to explain its meaning. It will be recalled that in the first scene of *The Sign of the Four* Holmes was bored because he had no problems to solve; "give me the most abstruse cryptogram." Another sign of *The Sign of the Four* is the association with the roof: "Roof Seckesign van der Deckel" (German, *Deckel*—lid).

(324.21) "Ellers for the greeter glossary of code, callen hom." All for the greater glory of God, and for a glossary of this code, call in Holmes.

Cryptography is the most important element in Holmes's case of *The Dancing Men*. The client, Mr. Hilton Cubitt, had married an American girl of unknown antecedents. They lived together very happily for a year, but one morning a strange cryptographic message was found on the sundial in Cubitt's garden. The message terrified Mrs. Cubitt and destroyed their happiness—like the serpent in the Garden of Eden.

(89.31–90.16) "That a head in thighs under a bush at the sunface would bait a serpent to a millrace through the heather. Arm bird colour defdum ethnic fort perharps? ... pigeegeeses? On a pontiff's order as ture as there's an ital.... But, why this hankowchaff and whence this second tone, son-yet-sun? ... the king's head to the republican's arms ... fatherthyme's beckside.... The devoted couple was or were only two disappainted."

The dancing men (head in thighs) found on the sundial (sunface) represented an unknown language—like the secret ogham alphabet invented by the Gaelic deity Ogma (Sun-face).[2] Bird calls, deaf and dumb signs, harp music? Portuguese, pig Latin, Italian? But it looks like a Chinese ideograph and it may be a joke (hankowchaff). The message found on the sundial was the second one (second tone, son-yet-sun) received by the Cubitts. The devoted couple had a happy British-American marriage (the king's head to the republican's arms).

Holmes cracked the code of the dancing men and sent off a cable to "my friend, Wilson Hargreave, of the New York Police Bureau.... I asked him whether the name of Abe Slaney was known to him. Here is his reply: 'The most dangerous crook in Chicago.' " (90.26–27) "The rudacist rotter in Roebuckdom ... in yappanoise language." Chicago (Roebuckdom) was headquarters for Sears Roebuck.

(26.15–23) "The loamsome roam to Laffayette is ended. Drop in your tracks, babe! Be not unrested! The headboddylwatcher of the chempel of Isis, Totumcalmum, saith: I now thee....For we have performed upon thee, thou abramanation, who comest ever without being invoked, whose coming is unknown, all the things which the company of the precenters and of the grammarians of Christpatrick's ordered concerning thee in the matter of thy tombing."

The reference to Lafayette evokes an American in Europe (Pershing's "Lafayette we are here!"). Holmes as "Totumcalmum" points out the similarity of the dancing men to Egyptian hieroglyphics, and "headboddyly watcher" combines the cryptogram and Sickerson, HCE's bottle washer. Abe Slaney (abramanation) was tricked (performed upon) and arrested (not unrested) by means of a false dancing men message composed by Holmes. " 'Well, gentlemen, you have the drop on me,' said Abe Slaney [Drop in your tracks, babe!]. 'There was no one on earth outside the Joint who knew the secret of the dancing men. How came you to write it?... He was a clever man was old Patrick. It was he who invented that writing' " (the grammarians of Christpatrick's').

" 'What one man can invent another can discover,' said Holmes."

The final *FW* reference to *The Dancing Men* seems to be on page 90. Four pages later we find Holmes again involved with a cryptogram. This time it is the Mamafesta in the form of a cipher.

(94.10–22) "The old hunks on the hill read it to perlection ...

What was it?
A...........!
?...........0!

"So there you are now ... when all was over again, the four with them ... under the suspices of Lally."

The case of *The Sign of the Four* is over for Lally. *The Valley of Fear* began with a cipher message from a Moriarty gangster turned informer, Fred Porlock. Holmes read the message as *FW* says "to perlection" (porlock plus perfection plus perlectio; Latin, read through).[3] Moriarty was suspicious (suspices) of Porlock.
What was it?

534 C2 13 127 36 31 4 17 21 41
DOUGLAS 109 293 5 37 BIRLSTONE
26 BIRLSTONE 9 127 171

The message was concealed in the numbered words on a specific page of a book, *Whitaker's Almanac*:

" 'There is danger—may—come—very—soon—one.' Then we have the name 'Douglas—rich—country—now—at—Birlstone—House—Birlstone—confidence—is pressing.' "

" 'What a queer, scrambling way of expressing his meaning!' said [Watson].

" 'On the contrary, he has done quite remarkably well,' said Holmes. 'When you search a single column for words with which to express your meaning, you can hardly expect to get everything you want. You are bound to leave something to the intelligence of your correspondent.' "

Holmes cited two cardinal rules in cryptography: leave something to the intelligence of the reader, and what one man can invent another can discover. And Joyce offers the same advice to readers of *FW*: (304.F3) "Wipe your glosses with what you know."

Which brings us to the identification of Sherlock Holmes as "the old hunks." The *Oxford English Dictionary* defines "hunks" as "a surly, crusty, crossgrained old person, a 'bear.' " When Holmes was a practicing detective, inactivity made him as surly as a bear, and he had sought relief in cocaine and morphine. But when he retired as an old man, he found a better remedy—honey. As is well known, bears love honey above all things. So the beekeeping, honey-loving Holmes is identified as (530.22) "Sackerson," a captive bear in the Paris Garden, near the Globe Theatre in Elizabethan London. In *Ulysses* Stephen Dedalus describes a Shakespearean performance at the Globe: (*U* 188) "The bear Sackerson growls in the pit near it, Paris garden." Another contemporary captive bear was named Harry Hunks.

(471.30–31) "Sickerson, that borne of bjoerne, la garde auxiliare she murmured, hellyg Ursulinka." Norwegian *bjorn*, and Latin *ursus*—bear; a chained bear (Ursulinka). Cf. Shakespeare, *The Merry Wives of Windsor*, I, i: slender: "You are afraid, if you see the bear loose, are you not?... I have seen Sackerson loose twenty times, and have taken him by the chain."

NOTES

1. Cf. Dickens, *Pickwick Papers*, Chapter 33. "Call Elizabeth [lizzy] Cluppins ... Elizabeth Tuppins ... Elizabeth Jupkins ... Elizabeth Muffins." In the trial of *Bardell vs Pickwick* a "letter" reading in full, "Chops and Tomata sauce" is offered as important evidence.

2. Adaline Glasheen identifies the secret writing of Ogma (Sun-face) in this passage. See *A Second Census of Finnegans Wake* (Evanston, Ill.: Northwestern University Press, 1963), 191.

3. Cf. Coleridge, whose cryptic poem, *Kubla Khan* begins with "Alph, the sacred river" and ends with "a circle round him thrice." The composition of the poem was interrupted by "a person from Porlock."

Chapter 6

The Adventure of Black Peter

The third paragraph of the story emphasizes its significance in *FW*. Watson writes:

> During the first week of July my friend had been absent so often and so long from our lodgings that I knew he had something on hand. The fact that several rough-looking men called during that time and inquired for Captain Basil made me understand that Holmes was working somewhere under one of the numerous disguises and names with which he concealed his own formidable identity. He had at least five small refuges in different parts of London in which he was able to change his personality.

(578.13–14) "He's the dibble's own doges for doublin existents!"

The "Black Peter" of the title was a retired whaling and sealing captain, Peter Carey, who was found murdered. Carey's ship, the *Sea Unicorn*, was cruising off the coast of Norway prior to the murder. In *FW*, the figures of Captain Peter and Captain Basil merge, and Sherlock Holmes becomes the mysterious Norwegian Captain. A rationale may be found in the final sentence of "Black Peter" wherein Holmes, having solved the case, said to Inspector Stanley Hopkins: "If you want me for the trial my address and that of Watson will be somewhere in Norway—I'll send particulars later."

(374.31–32) "Basil and the two other men from King's Avenance." Holmes, Watson and Hopkins captured the murderer. Presumably, the first two returned from Norway to give King's (or Queen's) evidence at the trial.

As for the Norwegian Captain, he is a countryman of Sigerson the explorer. In fact, he is Sigerson, (530,20) "Roof Seckesign van der Deckel." Here Sigerson becomes Vanderdecken, Wagner's Flying Dutchman, who sailed to Norway to woo Senta, the daughter of another Norwegian captain. In "The Sign of the Four," Holmes appeared disguised as a "respectable master mariner" (nationality not specified), who insisted on speaking to "Mr Sherlock Holmes" himself. (389.36–390.1) "For the seek of Senders Newslaters." Perhaps this means "send particulars later" and "for the sake of Senta." In "Black Peter," and in *FW*, this "aged man clad in seafaring garb" is recognized as the Old Man of the Sea, Proteus, the all-seeing, all-knowing herdsman of sea-beasts, who changes his shape at will.

In Book IV of *The Odyssey* [1] Homer tells us how Telemachus, grown to manhood during the long absence of his father, Odysseus, leaves his home island of Ithaca to seek news from others who have returned from the Trojan War. He travels to Sparta, where Menelaus reigns again after eight years of wandering. Menelaus tells of his encounter with Proteus on the Egyptian island of Pharos. Proteus uses his shape-changing ability to escape capture. But once captured and held fast, he can be forced to impart information.

Menelaus was becalmed off Pharos for twenty days, for he had unknowingly offended the gods, who would give him no wind. Walking disconsolately along the beach one day, he meets the sea-nymph Eidothee, daughter of Proteus, who takes pity on Menelaus. She tells him he must capture Proteus and learn how he may return to Sparta. Eidothee offers to help Menelaus ambush and capture Proteus when the ancient one of the sea returns to Pharos with his herd of seals.

"So do thou choose diligently three of thy company, the best thou hast in thy decked ships. And I will tell thee all the magic arts of that old man." Eidothee then gives Menelaus and his three companions four newly flayed seal skins.

> She scooped lairs on the sea-sand and made us all lie down in order and cast a skin over each ... And at high day the ancient one came forth from the brine and found his fatted seals ... and first among the sea beasts he reckoned us, and guessed not there was guile ... Then we rushed upon him with a cry and cast our hands about him, nor did that ancient one forget his cunning. Now behold at the first he turned into a bearded lion, and thereafter into a snake, and a pard, and a huge boar, then he took the shape of running water, and of a tall and flowering tree. We the while held him close with steadfast heart.

Once Proteus realized that escape was not possible, he begrudgingly advised Menelaus to offer a burnt sacrifice to the gods who would grant him favorable winds home. He also told Menelaus of the murder of Agamemnon and of the fate of Odysseus, who at that time was held prisoner on the island of Ogygia by the nymph Calypso.

In "Black Peter," we may identify Telemachus immediately. He is the questing John Hopley Neligan, seeking news of a father lost at sea. Holmes himself, the master of disguise, is an obvious Proteus. But as the story progresses, Proteus subtly imparts some aspects of himself to other characters as well.

For the murdered Peter Carey also shares something of Proteus. As a former whaling and sealing captain, Black Peter had been a herder of sea beasts. And he had been harpooned like a captured sea beast and "pinned like a beetle on a card," suggesting change into another animal. Furthermore, Peter Carey's daughter "blessed the hand which had struck him down," an unfilial attitude rather stronger than that of Eidothee, who merely betrayed Proteus to Menelaus.

(332.30–32) "As if she ever cared an assuan damm about her harpoons sticking all out of him whet between phoenix his calipers and that psourdonome sheath." Carey was found with a steel harpoon driven through his breast and "sunk deep into the wood of the all behind him." The harpoon was fixed in the wood like the sword Excalibur was fixed in the stone. The word "calipers" also suggests the mandibles of a beetle. The pseudonym, "Captain Basil," used for concealment, is suggested by "psourdonome sheath." The allusion is also to a sealskin tobacco pouch left behind by the murderer, Patrick Cairns. Since the pouch was initialled "P.C." it was mistakenly assumed to have been the property of Peter Carey.

In addition to "Black Peter," there are also suggestions of an Egyptian locale, identifying Proteus's Island of Pharos: the Assuan Dam on the Nile, the Phoenix, an Egyptian bird, and the scarab beetle. The Phoenix and the scarab beetle are symbols of immortality, echoing Odyssean references to "the immortal gods." Finally, the "psourdonome sheath" recalls the sour-smelling seal skins under which Menelaus and his companions concealed themselves.

(324.4–10) "Picking up the emberose of the lizod lights, his tail toiled of spume and spawn, and the bulk of him, and the hulk of him as whenever it was he reddled a ruad to riddle a rede from the sphinxish pairc while Ede was a guardin, ere love a side issue. They hailed him cheeringly, their encient, the murrainer, and wallruse, the merman, ye seal that lubs you lassers, Thallasee or Tullafilmagh when come of uniform age."

Here are allusions to the Ambrose Light, suggesting the lighthouse on the island of Pharos; the ambrosia, which Eidothee set beneath each man's nostrils to allay the stench of the sealskins beneath which they were hiding; Proteus himself coming up from the sea; the questions asked of him in Egypt (sphinxish); Eidothee (Ede) guarding Menelaus from harm, although she was the issue of Proteus (a side issue); that lubber, *Ulysses* (you lassers); (*Thallassa* the Greek word for sea; Telemachus (Tullafilmagh perhaps a combination with French *fils* for son) who was not yet of military (uniform) age.

In "Black Peter," there are two ambushes reminiscent of the ambush of Proteus. The first involved Holmes, Watson, and Hopkins, the Scotland Yard man, waiting for an unknown intruder to appear at Black Peter's cabin. Watson speculated: "What savage creature was it which might steal upon us out of the darkness? Was it a fierce tiger of crime ... or would it prove to be some skulking jackal?"

The animals suggest Proteus who, when captured, turned himself into a "bearded lion, and thereafter into a snake, and a pard and a huge boar." Certainly no tiger, the captured John Hopley Neligan meekly revealed everything he knew to Sherlock Holmes.

(26.2–4) "But as Hopkins and Hopkins puts it you were the pale eggynaggy and a kis to tilly up. We calls him the journeyall Buggaloffs since he went Jerusalemfaring in Arsia Manor."

"Hopkins and Hopkins" equals Hopkins and Hopley. Neligan was "the pale eggynaggy." His face had a "deadly pallor" and Hopkins theorized that he was "horrified by what he had done." The "agenbite of inwit," the twinge of conscience, identifies Stephen Dedalus, the Telemachus of *Ulysses* (*U* 16). In the Irish dialect, a "tilly" is something added for good measure, as the thirteenth bun in a baker's dozen. A "kist" is an ancient Arabic liquid measure. In the "Telemachus" episode of *Ulysses* (*U* 13), the old milkwoman "poured again a measureful and a tilly." It might be added that like Stephen Dedalus, John Hopley Neligan is also a Hamlet type. Neligan was incapable of avenging the murder of his father by killing Black Peter. "Do you imagine that this anaemic youth was capable of so frightful an assault?" asked Holmes.

Neligan is identified with Kersse the tailor, who made a suit of clothes for the Norwegian Captain (kis to tilly). Vasily Buslaevitch (Buggaloffs) was a legendary Russian seafarer—Captain Basil. (23.10–11) "How kirssy the tiler made a sweet unclose to the Narwhealian captol." Neligan made a complete disclosure to Sherlock Holmes (narwhale: *Sea Unicorn*). Perhaps the "journeyall Buggaloffs" also refers to the journal, the ship's log of the *Sea Unicorn*, which Neligan consulted. And it may include Neligan's father who went off on a journey and was thought to have absconded (buggered off). (622.25) "The Wald Unicorns Master, Bugley Captain from the Naul." Peter Carey built himself a cabin in the "weald" (Doyle's word).

(496.30–33) "He sent out Christy Columb and he came back with a jailbird's unbespokables in his beak and then he sent out Le Caron crow and the peacies are still looking for him. The seeker from the swayed, the beesabouties from the parent swarm."

Young Neligan was as innocent as a dove (Columb). Nevertheless, he was brought before a magistrate (beak) and jailed. A hint of Kersse the tailor appears in "unbespokables." The name "Cairns" can be seen (Caron). P.C.'s (peacies) are police constables as well as the initials on the "swayed" tobacco pouch. "Holmes the busybody! Mr. Busybody Holmes!" (beesabouties) were epithets known to criminals. And in later life Holmes kept himself busy with bees.

In preparation for the second ambush of the real murderer, Patrick Cairns, Holmes sent a telegram: "Sumner, Shipping Agent, Ratcliff Highway. Send three men on to arrive tomorrow morning—Basil." The three men were to be ostensibly recruited for a whaling and seal hunting expedition. In preparation for the ambush of Proteus, Menelaus recruited three men of his company to conceal themselves under seal skins. When Holmes slipped the handcuffs on Cairns, the captive gave "a bellow like an enraged bull," and there was a terrible struggle to hold him. But finally Cairns gave up and spoke freely, answering all questions.

Like the obstinate Proteus himself, the "Homework" chapter yields a wealth of information when captured. (263.1–16)

That same erst crafty hakemouth which under the assumed name of Ignotus Loquor, of foggy old, harangued bellyhooting fishdrunks on their favorite stamping ground, from a father theobalder brake.[1] And Egyptus, the incenstrobed, as Cyrus heard of him? And Major A. Shaw after he got the miner smellpex? And old Whiteman self, the blighty blotchy, beyond the bays ... despair of Pandemia's post-wartem plastic surgeons? ... not a feature alike and the face the same.[2]

Various elements of the Proteus myth appear in the body text as well as in the footnotes. "Ignotus Loquor" (ignorant blabbermouth) seems to be an antonym for the omniscient but silent Proteus. "Egyptus, Cyrus, Major A. Shaw and Whiteman" are probably Menelaus and his three companions come ashore (A. Shaw) under the smelly seal pelts (smellpex).

Footnote 1. "Huntler and Pumar's animal alphabites, the first in the world from aab to zoo."

Footnote 2. "We dont hear the booming cursowarries, we wont fear the fletches of fightning, we float the meditarenias and come back to the isle we love in spice." The cassowary is a flightless Australian bird. The Trojan war was over, and Menelaus was returning to his home island.

(263 left margin)

"Mars speaking."
"Smith, no home."
"Non quod sed quiat."
"Hearasay in paradox lust."

The margin notes have been explicated as paraphrasing an incident in *The Sign of the Four*. Another, more obvious, interpretation is the cuckolding of Vulcan by Mars in Book VIII of *The Odyssey*. But a third reading may be found in Book IV.

Menelaus related that the Greeks lay hidden inside the Trojan horse when Helen came out and called to them. "Thrice thou didst go round about the hollow ambush and handle it, calling aloud on the chiefs of the Argives by name, and making thy voice like the voices of the wives of all the Argives." (Ma's speaking.)

Several of the Greeks wanted to answer, but Odysseus, knowing it was not this one, said—Quiet! (non quod sed quiat.)

Odysseus "stayed and held us there, despite our eagerness." (Hearasay in paradox lust.)

"Then all the other sons of the Acheans held their peace." (Smith, no home.)

(307.5–6) "Since our Brother Johnathan Signed the Pledge.(2)"

Footnote 2: "Wherry luke the whaled prophet in a spookeerie." The text carries an allusion to Jonathan Small and *The Sign of the Four* while the footnote includes Proteus, Captain Basil the whaler, and perhaps a hint of Conan Doyle's spiritualism.

(371.6–8) "Dour douchy was a sieguldson. He cooed that loud nor he was young. He cud bad caw nor he was gray Like wather parted from the say."

"Dour" is the descriptive *mot juste* for the stubborn, uncommunicative Proteus. During the struggle with Menelaus he "took the shape of running water" (douche). He was the son of Poseidon—sea god's son, as well as Sigerson. That Proteus cooed when he was young may refer to the fact that he once knew love; he begat Eidothee. He cawed like a sea gull and was caught when he was gray.

Concerning the first three episodes of *Ulysses*, Stuart Gilbert has remarked that the least precise Homeric recalls are those relating to Proteus. In episodes one and two, Telemachus and Nestor are at least clearly personified. For Proteus, Gilbert cites with certainty one line. " 'Disguises, clutched at, gone, not here.' There is here an unmistakable allusion to Proteus in the ineluctable grip of his captor." On the same page Gilbert notes the presence of "the cocklepickers with their dog, itself proteiform as the tidal margin of the bay."[2] Thus the personification of Proteus in *Ulysses* appears to be a mongrel dog who struts and frets briefly on two pages and then goes lolloping off into oblivion.

If Proteus is elusive in *Ulysses*, he is even more elusive in *FW* where, among all the gods and heroes of mythology who appear in various forms, Proteus long remained unidentified. Nevertheless, Joyce called *FW* (107.8) "the proteiform graph itself." In another context, Atherton points out that the French symbolists are present in *FW* but are never named, since "a major tenet of their creed was '*Nommer est etruire.*' "[3] (To name is to destroy.) It is suggested here that, with a similar design, Joyce took special pains to disguise the elusive Proteus. To recognize is to capture. Black Peter may be one of the adventures honored with a title as part of ALP's Mamafesta. (105.9–10) "*The Log of Anny to the Base All.*" (Basil) The log book of the *Sea Unicorn*, with some pages missing, is an element in the case. It has been suggested that Leopold Bloom (*U* 163) read *Black Peter* in the March 1904 issue of *The Strand* magazine.[4]

NOTES

1. S.H. Butcher and Andrew Lang, *The Odyssey of Homer—Done into English Prose* (New York: The Modern Library, n.d.), 53-58.
2. Stuart Gilbert, *James Joyce's Ulysses* (New York: Modern Library, 1952), 103-25.
3. James S. Atherton, *The Books at The Wake* (New York: Viking Press, 1960), 21.
4. Fritz Senn, "Carey Was His Name," *James Joyce Quarterly* XXIV (Winter 1987), 214-16.

Chapter 7

The Adventure of the Priory School

This is the Sherlockian counterpart of the story of the prankquean, related on *FW* pages 21 through 23 with frequently recurring references thereafter. As Joyce tells the story, the Prankquean was a female pirate named Grace O'Malley who came one night to the castle of the Earl of Howth, "Jarl van Hoother," seeking shelter and refreshment. When she was denied entrance, she kidnapped the Earl's two sons, Tristopher and Hilary. Joyce does not make it clear why the elder son was unhappy (Tristopher) and the younger son was cheerful (Hilary).

In Conan Doyle's version, the Duke of Holdernesse, estranged from his Duchess, also had two sons. The unhappy elder, James (Tristopher), was illegitimate and unacknowledged. He lived with his father as the Duke's private secretary under the name of James Wilder. The fortunate younger son, Arthur (Hilary), was heir to the dukedom and a student at the Priory School, "the best and most select preparatory school in England."

Since the Duke was guilty of an early sexual fall from grace, he was an HCE figure. The mistress of his youth, the deceased mother of James, was a ghostly prankquean. The Duke did not marry his first mistress because she was beneath his station. Like the prankquean, she was denied admittance to the nobleman's hall.[1] James was kidnapped spiritually by his mother, and (21.30) "he became a luderman" (German: blackguard). "He always had a taste for low company," said the Duke. Arthur was kidnapped physically from the Priory School by James and an accomplice. The estranged Duchess (21.20–21) "her grace o' malice" was suspected at first, but the case was solved triumphantly by Sherlock Holmes. (23.11) "A sweet unclose to the Narwhealian captol." The Duke paid a handsome fee to Holmes, who was identified with the Norwegian captain in *The Adventure of Black Peter*.

Aside from the cryptic mention of Holmes, there is nothing in the first narration of the prankquean story to evoke *The Priory School*. Allusions to the plot may be noted several times when the story is told again in HCE's pub, on pages 335 through 77. Sherlock Holmes is not included in these later allusions, neither in person nor in disguise.

(335.30–31) "When Aimee stood for Arthurduke for the figger in profane and fell from grace so madley." There may be a hint here (Aimee) of the Duke's first profane love. (336.1–2) "And it was cyclums cyclorums after he made design on the corse." First, there is an allusion to *The Sign of the Four*, the earlier case. After that came *The Priory School,* which involved two bicycles (cyclums cyclorums), with tires of different make, so that the tire tracks (design on the course) were significant. Also, the tracks led to a corpse (corse).

(375.6–8) "Be blasted to bumboards by the youthful herald who would once you were. He'd be our chosen one in the matter of Brittas more than anarthur." This seems to be addressed to the Duke: James would be heir to the dukedom as once you were. He'd be chosen rather than Arthur.

(375.17–18) "One bully son growing the goff and his twinger read out by the Nazi Priers." When Arthur left the Priory School during the night, he was observed and followed by the German master, Heidegger, who was murdered. Martin Heidegger was the German Existentialist, Rector (Prior) of Freiburg University, who was able to accommodate his Philosophy to Nazism and serve Hitler.[2] It should be noted that this association of "Nazi Priers" with Martin Heidegger and the murdered German master is really strong evidence of the presence of *The Priory School* in *FW*. To my knowledge no commentator on *FW* has been able to offer a convincing alternative reading for "Nazi Priers." Fortunately, the identification is confirmed two pages later. (377.9–10) "Slip on your ropen collar and draw the noosebag on your head. Nobody will know or heed you, Postumus, if you skip round schlymartin by the back." This is James persuading his younger brother (Postumus) to put his head in a noose by slipping out of school. Heidegger the German master is called "schlymartin" in *FW,* although his actual Christian name is never mentioned in the Holmes story. In the original Latin *postumus* meant simply a younger or last-born child, not necessarily one associated with paternal death.[3]

(376.2–3) "Only but she is a little width wider got. Be moving abog. You cannot make a limousine lady out of a hillman minx." This is another allusion to the Duke's indiscretion. James's mother was "a little width wider," with Wilder.

Another reference appears as one in the list of dubious gifts, occupying more than two pages, bestowed on her numerous children by ALP, in her incarnation as Mother Eve. (211.26–28) "A guillotine shirt for Reuben Redbreast and hempen suspendeats for Brennan on the Moor." Reuben Hayes, landlord of the Fighting Cock Inn, and James Wilder's accomplice in the kidnapping of young Arthur, was arrested for the murder on the moor, and Holmes promised that he would go to the gallows. In a cock-fight the breasts of the combatants are usually red with blood and the identification with Reuben Hayes seems clear. The association with the redbreasted robin is also relevant. It relates to the concepts of original sin, Cain and Abel, and the wren as a crucifixion symbol which appear elsewhere in *FW*.[4]

Robert Graves points out that the Wren is killed by "the New Year Robin on St. Stephen's Day,"[5] and Frazer quotes a line sung on the Isle of Man as part of the annual Wren crucifixion ceremony: "We hunted the Wren for Robin the Bobbin"[6] The original sin of the Duke of Holdernesse, who "fell from grace so madley," led to the rivalry between his sons, culminating in the death of Heidegger. The German master, dying on the moor for the Duke's sin, is the Wren, "B(renn)an on the Moor." *Brennan on the Moor* is also the title of an Irish ballad about a highwayman who was hanged, becoming a type of martyred Robin Hood.

An added complexity appears in the hanging of Hayes. Like the Duke, whose sin was sexual, Hayes, as a guilty innkeeper, was an HCE figure. But the Duke escaped punishment for himself and for his bastard son by purchasing Hayes's silence. The latter assumed sole responsibility for the crime, thus becoming another scapegoat wren. (375.20–21) "When hives the court to exchequer 'tis the child which gives the sire away." As the Duke protected his son with money, so Hayes accepted his fate—presumably for the sake of his own children.

(599.4–9) "See you not soo the pfath they pfunded, oura vatars that arred in Himmal, ... mid trefoils slipped the sable rampant, hoof, hoof, hoof, hoof, padapodopudupedding on fattafottafutt."

"Can you recall that the tracks were sometimes like that, Watson"—he arranged a number of breadcrumbs in this fashion— : : : :—"and sometimes like this—: : : :—"and occasionally like this"— ... "Can you remember that?"

That was Holmes discussing the strange appearance of the cow tracks on the moor—another design on the course. Sets of antique horseshoes were kept in Holdernesse Hall in a glass case along with an inscription: "These shoes were dug up in the moat of Holdernesse Hall. They are for the use of horses, but they are shaped below with a cloven foot of iron, so as to throw pursuers off the track. They are supposed to have belonged to some of the marauding Barons of Holdernesse in the Middle Ages." The *FW* passage includes the duke's marauding ancestors (oura vatars that arred) and the family heraldic device (trefoils ... sable rampant).

"Holmes opened the case, and moistening his finger he passed it along the shoe. A thin film of recent mud was left upon his skin." (599.10–11) "The emplacement of solid and fluid having to a great extent persisted."

NOTES

1. The Duke's treatment of his pregnant mistress is reminiscent of an old ballad, "The Lass of Aughrim," which Joyce especially liked: "My babe lies cold within my arms; Lord Gregory, let me in." Lord Gregory refuses and the lass drowns herself. In his short story "The Dead" (*Dubliners*), Joyce has Bartell D'Arcy singing these very lines. See Richard Ellmann, *James Joyce* (New York: Oxford University Press, 1959), 257, 295.

2. Walter Kaufmann, *Existentialism from Dostoevsky to Sartre* (New York: Meridian Books, 1956) 34: "Heidegger's enthusiastic exhortations, shortly after Hitler came to power, that the students and professors at the German universities must now think in the service of the Nazi state—his inaugural address as Rektor at Freiburg has been printed."

3. The *Oxford English Dictionary* defines: "Posthumous . . . f. L. *postumus*, last, late-born. . . . in late L. written *posthumus* through erroneous attribution to *humus* the earth, or (as explained by Servius) *humare* to bury."

4. Joseph Campbell and Henry Morton Robinson, *A Skeleton Key to Finnegans Wake* (New York: Viking Press, 1961), 62: " 'The Wren, the Wren, the King of all Birds, St. Stephen's Day was caught in the furze.' A traditional verse sung on St. Stephen's Day when a wren is killed and carried about town on a stick. This Scapegoat Wren is a folk reduction of the crucified god and as such . . . runs through many pages of *Finnegans Wake*."

5. Robert Graves, *The White Goddess* (New York: Vintage Books, 1958), 92.

6. James George Frazer, *The New Golden Bough*, Ed. Theodor H. Gaster (New York: New American Library, 1959), 561–62.

Chapter 8

The Man with the Twisted Lip

The case of a man suspected of murdering himself is a Sherlockian counterpart of the Trial of Festy King, one of the most enigmatic episodes in *FW* (81–93). Apparently Festy King has committed an offense of some sort, but it may not be an actual crime, and the identity of the key witness is uncertain. It turns out that the witness, Pegger Festy, and the accused Festy King, are the same person. The case is so confusing that the verdict is an inconclusive (93.1) "Nolans Brumans:" the Latin *nolens nolens* (willy-nilly) plus the Nolan Bruno. The philosopher Giordano Bruno, of Nola, Italy, preached the doctrine of the unity of opposites.

The Sherlock Holmes adventure concerns the disappearance of Neville St. Clair, a supposedly respectable man of business who had for years been making a comfortable living as a deformed beggar, a man with a twisted lip. The beggar, arrested for the murder of the missing St. Clair, was literally unmasked by Sherlock Holmes—with two strokes of a bathroom sponge. Perhaps Doyle's feisty beggar is Joyce's Pegger Festy. In any case, nobody has attempted another explication of the name "Pegger."

(81.16–20) "(Benathere! Benathere!) but where livland yontide meared with the wilde, saltlea with flood, that the attackler, ... between colours with truly native pluck, engaged the Adversary, who had more in his eye than was less to his leg." The disreputable lodging of the beggar overlooked a "narrow strip, which is dry at low tide, but is covered at high tide with at least four and a half feet of water." A ghat on the Ganges at Benares (Benathere) is suggested by the house and by the landlord, who was a "rascally lascar" (between colours, truly native). At Benares in India, the River Ganges washes away the ashes of cremated Hindus. Similarly, the tide in the Thames was thought to have washed away the body of Neville St. Clair. The beggar had a crippled leg (less to his leg) and "a pair of very penetrating dark eyes" (more in his eye).

(81.31–33) "Catching holst of an oblong bar he had and with which he usually broke furnitures.... The boarder incident prerepeated itself." The beggar was a boarder on the premises of an opium den called the Bar of Gold (oblong bar), which was visited repeatedly (prerepeated) by Isa Whitney, a friend of Watson's. Opium addiction was breaking up Whitney's home (broke furnitures).

(85.23–27) "Festy King, of a family long and honorably associated with the tar and feather industries, who gave an address in the heart of a foulfamed potheen district, was subsequently haled up at the Old Bailey ... under an incompatibly framed indictment." Watson described the lodging where Neville St. Clair assumed the identity of the beggar: "Upper Swandam Lane is a vile alley lurking behind the high wharves which line the north side of the river ... Between a slop-shop and a gin-shop [foulfamed potheen district] ... I found the den."

(86.7–11) Festy King "elois Crowbar, ... rubbed some pixes of any luvial peatsmoor o'er his face, plucks and pussas, with a clanetourf as the best means of disguising himself." (82.23–26) "His change companion who stuck still to the invention of his strongbox, with a tenacity corrobberating their mutual tenitorial rights, happened to have the loots change of a tenpound crackler about him." The passages refer to a change of identity and to the fact that the beggar's loot consisted of a heavy (tenpound) quantity of small change. The beggar and his lascar landlord (mutual tenitorial rights) told corroborating stories and stuck to them with tenacity.

(90.34–91.4) "But a new complexion was put upon the matter when ... the senior king of all, Pegger Festy, as soon as the outer layer of stucckomuck had been removed at the request of a few live jurors, declared ... on his oath." (83.5–9) "Which at very first wind of gay gay and whiskwigs ... the starving gunman....sware by all his lards porsenal that ... he would go good." Holmes washed the beggar's face and whisked off his red wig (whiskwigs). St. Clair vowed to reform. "I have sworn it by the most solemn oaths which a man can take." Macaulay's "Lars Porsena of Clusium,/ By the nine gods he swore" (lards porsenal).[1]

(81.22–23) "Parr aparrently, to whom the headandheelless chickenestegg bore some Michelangiolesque resemblance." A possible allusion to Michelangelo's statue *Perseus* [Parr?] *with the Head of Medusa* would be appropriate. The beggar's "hideous aspect" was Medusa-like. He also wore a heavy wig, "a twitch brought away the tangled red hair," which Holmes held aloft—like the severed head of the Gorgon. Perhaps Joyce thought that the de-wigged man might be as bald as a "chickenestegg." Actually, Watson observed that St. Clair had dark hair.

(82.16–18) "We at once recognize our old friend Ned of so many illortemporate letters." Neville St. Clair wrote a hurried note to his wife: "Dearest, do not be frightened. All will come well. ... It may take some little time to rectify." (82.19–20) "Did the inmage of Girl Cloud Pensive flout above them light young charm in ribbons and pigtail." Mrs. St. Clair was "a little blond woman ... clad in some sort of light *mousseline de soie*, with a touch of fluffy pink chiffon at her neck and wrists."

Somebody at the bar in HCE's pub told the story later. (325.33–34) "And no more of your maimed acts after this with your kowtoros and criados to every tome, thick and heavy." The feisty beggar had been "ever ready with a reply to any piece of chaff which may be thrown at him by the passers-by" (*criado* is Spanish for manservant).

The gossip about Neville St. Clair as Festy King was even discussed by Shem, Shaun and Issy when they should have been doing their homework. (290.12–21) "Gave him then that vantage of a Blinkensope's cuddlebath at her proper mitts ... doubling back in nowtime, (5) bymby when saltwater he wush him ... (would it wash;) with a cheek white peaceful as, wen shall say, a single professed claire's (6)." (290.F5) "The Wreck of the Ragamuffin." (290.F6) "No wonder Miss Dotsh took to veils." Perhaps footnote six means that Mrs. St. Clair thought she was a widow.

A set of child's building blocks was a clue in the case, which may have given it a Mamafesta title. (106.14) "*A Pretty Brick Story for Childsize Heroes*."

NOTE

1. Thomas Babington Macauley, poem, "Horatius at the Bridge," in *Lays of Ancient Rome*.

(*FW* 15.29–30) This carl on the kopje in pelted thongs a parth a lone who the joebiggar be he?

(16.33–34) the intellible greytcloak of Cedric Silkyshag!

(17.13) Boildoyle and rawhoney on me. . . .

(609.35–36) An I would uscertain in druidful scatterings one piece tall chap he stand one piece same place?

"Night had settled upon the moor." Illustration by Frederic Dorr Steele. In "The Man on the Tor" in *The Hound of the Baskervilles*. From Sir Arthur Conan Doyle, *The Later Adventures of Sherlock Holmes* (New York: Heritage Press, 1952).

Chapter 9

The Hound of the Baskervilles

"You interest me very much, Mr. Holmes. ...I had hardly expected so dolichocephalic a skull or such a well-marked supra-orbital development. A cast of your skull, sir, until the original is available, would be an ornament to any anthropological museum. It is not my intention to be fulsome, but I must confess that I covet your skull." The speaker was Dr. James Mortimer of Grimpen, Dartmoor, Devonshire, medical officer for the parishes of Grimpen, Thorsley and High Barrow and an enthusiastic amateur anthropologist.

(530.21) "Recall Sickerson the lizzyboy. Seckerson, magnon of Errick." Cromagnon man, whose remains were discovered in a cave near the town of Les Eyzies in France, had a skull larger than that of modern man. Both "lizzyboy" and "magnon" refer appropriately to Sherlock Holmes's skull.

There are many references to prehistoric man in *The Hound of the Baskervilles*. In that part of Devonshire near Baskerville Hall, "you are conscious everywhere of the homes and the work of prehistoric people. ... As you look at their grey stone huts against the scarred hillsides you leave your own age behind you, and if you were to see a skin-clad hairy man crawl out from a low door, ... you would feel that his presence there was more natural than your own." So Watson described the locale.

But Dr. James Mortimer had not come to Baker Street to discuss anthropology. The doctor was greatly disturbed by the mysterious circumstances surrounding the death of Sir Charles Baskerville. To Dr. Mortimer, these circumstances recalled the legend of the curse put upon the Baskerville family in the seventeenth century, when Sir Hugo Baskerville had died violently. "Plucking at his throat, there stood a foul thing, a great black beast, shaped like a hound yet larger than any hound that ever mortal eye had rested upon. And even as they looked the thing tore the throat out of Hugo Baskerville." So the legend was told in an old family manuscript in Dr. Mortimer's possession.

There had been no marks of violence on the body of the late Sir Charles Baskerville, descendent of Hugo. But Sir Charles was found after midnight, "his arms out, his fingers dug into the ground and his features convulsed with some strong motion," in the alley of yew trees on his estate. Except for Sir Charles's own footprints, the only marks on the ground near the body were "the footprints of a gigantic hound." Dr. Mortimer also remembered Sir Charles's look of horror on a recent occasion when they both saw what the doctor "took to be a large black calf passing at the head of the drive."

Here are excerpts from a newspaper account of the death of Sir Charles: " 'There is no reason whatever to suspect foul play, or to imagine that death could be from any but natural causes. ... In spite of his considerable wealth he was simple in his personal tastes... .

" 'The facts of the case are simple. ... That night he went out as usual for his nocturnal walk....He never returned ... death from cardiac exhaustion. This explanation was borne out by the post-mortem examination which showed long-standing organic disease, and the corner's jury returned a verdict in accordance with the medical evidence.' "

(291.F8) "Charles de Simples had an infirmierity complex before he died a natural death." But Sir Charles's death was neither simple nor entirely natural. He had been a childless widower, and his death had been planned and induced by an unrecognized nephew, the second in line to inherit the baronetcy and the estate of Baskerville. (291.27–28) "As though he, a notoriety, a foist edition, were a regular writher neonovene babe! (8)" The body text on *FW* 291 suggests an insect larva. A caterpillar would be most relevant because the unacknowledged Baskerville was a lepidopterist. Clear and amusing allusions occur elsewhere in the "Night Lessons" chapter.

(262.13–14)

When shoo, his flutterby,
Was netted and named (4).

The murderer, Rodger Baskerville, called himself Stapleton in Devonshire. He had previously used the name Vandeleur. "The name of Vandeleur has been permanently attached to a certain moth which he had, in his Yorkshire days, been the first to describe." (262.F4) "Apis amat aram. Luna legit librum. Pulla petit pascua."

Eugene Aram, like Stapleton, was a murderer and one-time Yorkshire schoolmaster. As an entomologist Stapleton loved bees (Apis amat aram), an interest he shared with Sherlock Holmes. The Luna is a species of moth, and Holmes had read of the Vandeleur species in the library of the British Museum (Luna legit librum). Stapleton planned an eventual resurrection of himself as Rodger Baskerville (Pulla petit pasucua. *Pascua* equals Spanish "Easter"). The Spanish word is significant since Stapleton had been born in South America.

(262.20–24) "Staplering to tether to, steppingstone to mount by, as the Boote's at Pickardstown. And that skimmelk steed still in the groundloftfan ... beastskin trophies. (7)." Stapleton kept his hound accomplice confined with a "staple and chain" in an abandoned mine shaft located in the middle of the Great Grimpen Mire. The mine could be reached only by walking carefully, as through a maze, on a faintly marked path (steppingstone). Also, since the murderer schemed to inherit the Baskerville estate, the name "Stapleton" was a "steppingstone to mount by." The hound was to identify the victim by the scent of a stolen boot. Fourteen miles from Baskerville Hall was the great prison of Princetown, where convicts at hard labor picked oakum (Pickardstown).[1] Stray moor ponies were often lost in the mire (groundloftfan), screaming (skimmelk? steed) as they went down. A pet spaniel had been eaten by the hound, leaving "a skeleton with a tangle of brown hair" (beastskin trophies).

(262, left margin) "*Tickets for the Tailwaggers Terrierpuppy Raffle.*" (right margin) "GNOSIS OF PRECREATE DETERMINATION. AGNOSIS OF POSTCREATE DETERMINISM." Stapleton's plans were not destined for success.

(262.F7) "Begge. To go to Begge. To go to Begge and be sure to reminder Begge. Goodbeg, buggey Begge." A similar passage occurs in an early chapter. (58.16–17) "Oho, oho, Mester Begge, you're about to be bagged in the bog again. Bugge." A typical command given a well-trained dog is "Beg!" "Goodbeg" may combine "Good Boy!" and "Goodbye," the latter word referring to the fate of

Stapleton who was eventually "bagged in the bog." "Bugge" and "buggey" of course refer to Stapleton as an entomologist.

(244.21) "Hound through the maize has fled." This may be another allusion to the maze through the bog which led to the kennel of the hound.

(287.5–6) "Take your mut for a first beginning, big to bog, back to bach." *The Oxford English Dictionary Supplement* defines: "Mutt, a term of contempt applied to a dog." *FW* (15–18) cover the Mutt and Jute encounter, which is strongly reminiscent of the *Hound* chapter entitled "The Man on the Tor." For the sake of brevity passages from both books will be synopsized.

Mutt, on his native heath, encounters a stranger. (15.29–35) "In the name of Anem this carl on the kopje in pelted thongs a parth a lone who the joebigger be he? Forshapen his pigmaid hoagshead … most mousterious. It is slaking nuncheon out of some thing's brain pan." The stranger seems to be a Mousterian cave man. He is drinking out of a skull. That the Mutt and Jute episode occurs in the Stone Age is consistent with Watson's description of the moor with its ancient stone huts and the "skin-clad hairy man" he imagined as an inhabitant (in pelted thongs).

(15.34–35) "He is almonths on the kiep fief by here, is Comestipple Sacksoun." The constable is off tippling sack as always. He's almost as bad as a hashish addict (on the kief pipe).

Watson had been spending several days at Baskerville Hall without Holmes, who was presumed to be back in London. Watson became aware of a stranger on the moor, a mysterious man on the tor (carl on the kopje), and tracked him to his hiding place in a partially ruined neolithic hut. The stranger turned out to be Sherlock Holmes.

Regretting the absence of the constable, Mutt approached the stranger who introduced himself as Jute. There was some conversation culminating in identification. (16.33–34) "Mutt—Louee, louee! How wooden I not know it, the intellible greytcloak of Cedric Silkyshag!"

"Intellible" combines "indelible" in the sense of "unforgettable" with tones of "unmentionable." The meaning suggested here is unforgettable but unmentioned cloak. Holmes's Inverness cloak is unforgettable, but it was never mentioned by Watson. The cloak was created by magazine illustrators, along with the deerstalker cap.

"Cedric" provides a possible association with "Comestipple Sacksoun" (Cedric the Saxon in Scott's *Ivanhoe*).

The shag in "Silkyshag" was the Master's favorite pipe tobacco. At an early point in the *Hound* he asked Watson, "When you pass Bradley's would you ask him to send up a pound of the strongest shag tobacco?" In the chapter of "The Man on the Tor" tobacco is a means of identification. Holmes knew that Watson was waiting inside the stone hut because a cigarette butt bearing "Bradley's" trademark was on the ground outside.

Mutt begins to tell Jute the history of the locale. Jute is impatient. (17.13–15) "Jute—Boildoyle and rawhoney on me when I can beuraly forsstand a weird from sturk to finnic in such a patwhat." Here are references to Doyle, bee keeping (rawhoney), the spectral hound (weird) and to language.

Holmes usually tended to denigrate Watson's published accounts of the cases. But in the *Hound* the Master expressed appreciation of Watson's written reports: "Here are your reports, my dear fellow, and very well thumbed, I assure you ... I must compliment you."

In the final chapter of *FW*, Mutt and Jute reappear as Muta and Juva.

(609.24–27) "*Muta*: Quodestnunc fumusiste volhvuns ex Domoyno?

"*Juva*: It is Old Head of Kettle puffing off the top of the mornin.

"*Muta*: He odda be thorly well ashamed of himself for smoking before the high host."

The Latin roughly translates as "What is that smoke now emanating from the Lord?" Holmes's devotion to tobacco received special emphasis in the *Hound*. "The room was so filled with smoke that the light of the lamp upon the table was blurred by it ... through the haze I had a vague vision of Holmes ... with his black clay pipe between his lips."

(609.35–36) "*Muta*: ... An I would uscertain in druidful scatterings one piece tall chap he stand one piece same place?" This is the second time that Mutt, or Muta, recognized the tall chap, Sherlock Holmes, standing among the ring of stones, the "druidful scatterings," perhaps resembling a smaller Stonehenge.

(186.19–21) "Petty Constable Sistersen of the Kruis-Kroon-Kraal it was, the parochial watch, big the dog the dig the bog the bagger the duggar the begadag degabug." The ancient structures on the moor were described as "grey circular rings of stone." Hence "Kruis-Kroon-Kraal" may be interpreted as "crude, ruined kraal," or enclosure.

(279.F1) "Wasn't it just divining that dog of a dag in Skokholme as I sat astrid uppum their Drewitt's altar ... offering me clouts of illscents." This seems to be another allusion to Holmes skulking in the ruins on a Druid's altar. (right margin) "MODES COALESCING PROLIFERATE HOMOGENUINE HOMOGENEITY."

(271.33–34) "*Left Boot Sent on Approval.*" This is one of a catalogue of abusive names directed at HCE in disgrace. It may also allude to Sir Henry's stolen boot, scented, for the approval of the hound.

(489.18–23) "He feels he ought to be asamed of me as me to be ashunned of him. We were in one class of age like to two clots of egg. I am most beholding to him, my namesick, as we sayed it in our Amharican, through the Doubly Telewisher. Outpassed hearts wag short pertimes. Worndown shoes upon his feet, to whose redress no tongue can tell! In his hands a boot!"

Sir Henry Baskerville, the rightful heir, had returned from Canada to claim the title. His cousin Rodger came from South America. They were both "Amharicans." Rodger had been passed over (outpassed). To seek redress he stole one of Sir Henry's boots to familiarize the fierce hound with the scent.

(489.27–28) "With the moonshane in his profile, my shemblable! My freer!" Among the ancestral portraits in Baskerville Hall was a painted likeness of the evil Sir Hugo. Holmes showed the painting to Watson. "He stood upon a chair, and holding up the light in his left hand, he curved his right arm over the broad hat and round the long ringlets.

" 'Good heavens!' I cried, in amazement.

"The face of Stapleton had sprung out of the canvas."

Mon semblable. Mon frère. (French—My double. My brother). This a quotation from *Fleurs du mal* (Flowers of Evil) by the French poet Charles Baudelaire.

(519.32–520.2) "Some rain was promised to Mrs. Lyons, the invalid of Aunt Tarty Villa. ... He is doing a walk, says she, in the feelmick's park, says he, like a tarrable Turk, says she, letting loose on his nursery."

Stapleton had promised marriage to Mrs. Laura Lyons, a woman of "equivocal reputation" deserted by her husband. She was persuaded to arrange a rendezvous with Sir Charles Baskerville in his park. Instead of Mrs. Lyons, Sir Charles met Stapleton's terrible Tyke (Hound), which had been let loose.

(449.10–11) "The nippy girl of my heart's appointment, Mona Vera Toutou Ipostila, my lady of Lyons, to guide me by gastronomy under her safe conduct. That's more in my line."

Mrs. Lyons was the lady of the posted letter (Ipostila) requesting an appointment. The rest of the passage raises the possibility that Joyce may have found a more venerable source for *The Hound of the Baskervilles* than the "West-Country legend" Doyle credits. The words "guide me ... under her safe conduct ... in my line" may allude to the myth of Theseus and Ariadne, wherein Ariadne guided Theseus in and out of the labyrinth by means of a spool of thread (in my line), thus enabling him to return safely after killing the Minotaur. Similarly, Stapleton's wife, Beryl, guided Holmes and Watson along the labyrinthine path to the hiding place of the Hound. Mrs. Lyons also was a twice-betrayed Ariadne figure: deserted by her husband, manipulated and deceived by Stapleton.[2]

NOTES

1. Cf. *Ulysses* wherein Leopold Bloom observed a man he decided was an ex-convict. (*U* 636) "Sherlockholmesing him up . . . it required no violent stretch of the imagination to associate such a weirdlooking specimen with the oakum and treadmill fraternity."

2. For other analogies between *The Hound of the Baskervilles* and the myth of Theseus and the Minotaur, see William D. Jenkins, "Have Sight of Proteus: Mythological Archetypes in the Sherlockian Canon," *Baker Street Journal*. 34, no. 3 (September 1984), 150–54.

Chapter 10

A Scandal in Bohemia

"To Sherlock Holmes she is always *the woman*. I have seldom heard him mention her under any other name. In his eyes she eclipses and predominates the whole of her sex. It was not that he felt any emotion akin to love for Irene Adler. All emotions, and that one particularly, were abhorrent to his cold, precise but admirably balanced mind. He was, I take it, the most perfect reasoning and observing machine that the world has seen, but as a lover he would have placed himself in a false position."

(310.20–21) "(the man of Iren, thore's Curlymane for you!), lill the lubberendth of his otological life." A Joycean evolution (Sherlock to Curleylock Curleymane) provides an association with Charlemagne, who declined a marriage with Empress Irene of Byzantium. Holmes was not only oh-so-logical, he was otological as well. He published two monographs on the variability of human ears (otology) in *The Anthropological Journal*.[1] His ability to resist feminine charm made him a man of iron, but despite himself he loved Irene till the end of his life. Joyce's "lill" suggests Lily Langtry, like Irene Adler, a one-time royal mistress.

A concentration of allusions appears on page 32, beginning with the visit of the king of Bohemia to Baker Street. His Majesty feared a scandal because of a compromising photograph in the possession of Irene Adler. Holmes was retained to retrieve the photo. (32.5–7) "This man is mountain and unto changeth doth one ascend. Heave we aside the fallacy, as punical as finikin, that it was not the king kingself." The king paid a personal call on Sherlock Holmes, his "slow and heavy step" sounding on the stairs. It was a case of the mountain coming to Mohammed. "I am not accustomed to doing such business in my own person," said the king. At first he wore a mask and introduced himself as "Count Von Kramm, a Bohemian nobleman," a finicky fallacy Holmes promptly heaved aside.

(32.9–11) "Robberers shot up the socialights ... Lily Miskinguette." Burglers in the pay of the king of Bohemia twice ransacked Irene Adler's house but were unable to find the damning photograph. Irene Adler, "born in New Jersey," is again identified with the other "Jersey Lily" and royal mistress, Lily Langtry. Of course she missed getting the king (miskinguette). (32.13–14) "All holographs ... bear the sigla H.C.E." The note, making an appointment with Holmes, was written in the king's own hand (holograph). Although it was unsigned, the paper was watermarked with "a large E with a small *g* a *P* and a large *G*." (32.19–24) "An imposing everybody he always indeed looked ... *Loots in his* (bassvoco) *Boots*." The king had a "deep harsh voice." His attire was opulent, his boots "trimmed at the top with rich brown fur." (32.29–35) "Mr Wallenstein ..., in a command performance ... for pious purposes the homedromed and enliventh performance of ... *A Royal Divorce* ... with ambitious interval band selections from *The Bo' Girl* and *The Lily*." Wallenstein was another "Bohemian nobleman," a seventeenth century soldier and statesman. Holmes remarked that he had died in the Bohemian town of "Egria" (Eger). With a supporting cast of accomplices, and himself in the role of a "Nonconformist clergyman" (for pious purposes), Holmes staged a small drama at the house of Irene Adler in order to gain admittance to find the compromising photograph. The opera, *The Bohemian Girl*, has double significance in that the plot involves lovers separated because the hero, Thaddeus, was not known to be of noble birth.

(68.19–23) "Missbrand her behaveyous with iridescent huecry of down right mean false sop lap sick dope? Tawfulsdreck! A reine of the shee, a shebeen quean, a queen of pranks. A kingly man, of royal mien, regally robed, exalted be his glory! So gave so take: Now not, not now!" In front of Irene's door Holmes staged a street brawl (huecry, pranks) and pretended to be injured (sick dope). He was carried into the house. Watson was "heartily ashamed of myself" (down right mean false) for his part in the deception. Teufelsdröckh is the philosopher of Carlyle's *Sartor Resartus*, Holmes again disguised.[2] Irene (A reine) appears, as well as the royal renege (so gave, so take).

Although there are many other possible allusions to *A Scandal in Bohemia* scattered through *FW*, there is only one more that seems certain. It occurs on the same page as the naming of "that Shedlock Homes Person." (165.15–16) "*The Very Picture of a Needlesswoman.*" The day after his illegal entry (Shedlock Homes) into the house of Irene Adler, Holmes returned to find that the lady had departed for the Continent but had left behind a letter for Holmes and a portrait of herself. The picture was intended for the king, but Holmes preferred it to an emerald ring. The king had no further need of Irene, and Holmes boasted that he had need of no woman. Nevertheless he cherished the picture.

A possible Mamafesta title: (106.12–13) "*Siegfeld Follies and or a Gentlehomme's Faut Pas.*" The king of Bohemia's Christian names and titles included "Sigismond ... Felstein" (Siegfeld). Holmes is also present (homme's).

NOTES

1. See *The Cardboard Box.*

2. "Tawfulsdreck" combines the image of Holmes wearing the clothes of a clergyman with Watson's guilty shame for his own part in the deception. Watson felt like an awful shit. *Teufelsdrockh* means devil's dung in German.

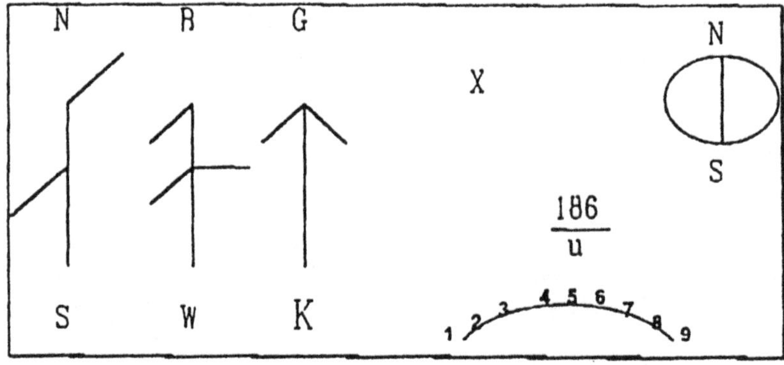

The Musgrave ritual. From James Joyce, *Finnegans Wake* (New York: Viking Press, 1939), 293.

Chapter 11

The Musgrave Ritual

In the Night Lessons chapter, Shem, Shaun and Issy do their homework. (306.12–15) "We've had our day at triv and quad and writ our bit as intermidgets. Art, literature, politics [ALP], economy, chemistry, humanity [ECH]." That the initials of the father are reversed signals the intent of the sons to overthrow him. Triv and quad are the two courses of medieval education: the *trivium*, primary (grammar, rhetoric, logic), and the *quadrivium*, advanced (arithmetic, music, geometry, astronomy). Appropriately, the curriculum in *FW* includes *The Musgrave Ritual,* which is helpful in learning mathematics, history, astronomy, logic, zoology and, of course, literature.

(293.23–25) "The Turnpike under the Great Ulm (with Mearingstone in Fore ground)." The ritual of the Musgrave family included these words: "Where was the shadow? Under the elm." The great elm had been cut down, but Reginald Musgrave remembered that it was exactly sixty-four feet in height. "When my old tutor used to give me an exercise in trigonometry it always took the shape of measuring heights. When I was a lad I worked out every tree and building on the estate." A path of many turnings (Turnpike) was described in the ritual: "North by ten and by ten, east by five and by five, south by two and by two, west by one and by one, and so under." Two other elements were the mere into which the Stuart crown and treasure had been thrown, and the "flagstone with a rusted iron ring in the centre" which gave access to an underground vault (Mearingstone in Fore ground).

(293.25–26) "Given now ann linch you take enn all." Holmes determined where the shadow of the felled elm would have fallen. "Of course, the calculation was now a simple one. If a rod of 6 feet threw a shadow of 9 feet, a tree of 64 feet would throw one of 96 feet." (293.26–28) "And heaving alljawbreakical expressions out of old Sare Isaac's (2) universal of specious aristmystic unsaid." Sir Isaac Newton's *Principia*; Sarah and her son Isaac, suggesting a family birthright, and finally, the mystic ritual of the aristocratic Musgraves (aristmystic).

(293.F2) "O, Laughing Sally, are we going to be toadhauntered by that old Pantifox Sir Somebody Something, Burtt, for the rest of our secret stripture?" *The Musgrave Ritual* is of course "our secret stripture?" Rachel Howells, the Musgrave housemaid, hysterically emitted "shriek after shriek of laughter" after she had immured Brunton the butler (Laughing Sally). Brunton was asphyxiated in the airless vault—where a toad would have survived for years, according to the popular superstition (toadhauntered).

"Pantifox" begins one of Joyce's portmanteau-word masterpieces. Zoologically speaking, it means a hunted fox run to earth and panting for breath in its burrow: like Brunton, clever as a fox, but gasping in the airless underground vault. A literary reference is to the Pontifex family, Theobald and Ernest, in *The Way of All Flesh*, by Samuel Butler —Brunton's profession. "Sir Somebody Something, Burtt" is an exercise in logic. If Bart is the abbreviation for Baronet, then Burtt should be the abbreviation for Buronett—an anagram for Brunton plus burrow net, an underground trap. (Cf. above: A rod of 6 feet : a tree of 64 feet :: a shadow of 9 feet: a shadow of X feet.) So much for mathematics, astronomy, zoology, literature and logic.

The historical aspect of *The Musgrave Ritual* recalls the Great Rebellion, Oliver Cromwell, the execution of Charles I and the Restoration of Charles II. The "old Pantifox Sir Somebody Something" is Reginald Musgrave's ancestor Sir Ralph Musgrave, "right-hand man of Charles II in his wanderings" and, in effect, pontifex to the Stuarts. According to the *Encyclopaedia Britannica* (11th ed.), the functions of the pontifex maximus in ancient Rome included the following: "administration of the law relating to burials and burying places, and the worship of the Manes, or dead ancestors … [and] the administration of the law of adoption and of testamentary succession.

The ritual "to which each Musgrave had to submit when he came to man's estate," concerned "nothing less than the ancient crown of the kings of England." During the Protectorate of Cromwell the crown had been hidden for safekeeping in a vault of the Musgrave ancestral house and forgotten. Holmes explained: "Consider what the Ritual says. How does it run? 'Whose was it?' 'His who is gone.' That was after the execution of Charles. Then 'Who shall have it?' 'He who will come.' That was Charles the Second, whose advent was already foreseen." The interregnum of Oliver Cromwell is noted on the second page of the Night Lessons chapter. (261, left margin) "*Cronwall beeswaxing the Convulsion Box.*" Cromwell's Puritans sealed up the confession boxes in England and Ulster, and the royal crown was walled up for safekeeping (Cronwall).

(287.9–11) "To find a locus for an alp get a howlth on her bayrings as a prisme O and for a second O unbox your compasses." (287, left margin) "*Wolsherwomens at their weirdst.*" Rachel Howells, the housemaid, "of an excitable Welsh temperament—had a sharp touch of brain fever." She was at her weirdest after burying (bayrings) Brunton in the vault. The butler had the help (alp) of Howells (howlth) in locating the lost crown. Rachel put the crown in a linen sack and threw it into the mere, like a washerwoman at a weir. Holmes mentioned that he had used his pocket compass to get his bearings in finding the hidden box.

(306.8–9) "But while the dial are they doodling dawdling over the mugs and the grubs?" (306, right margin) "ENTER THE COP AND HOW." While Reginald Musgrave and Brunton are "doodling dawdling" over the Musgrave Ritual (the mugs and the grubs), Sherlock Holmes enters from the right margin.

We leave the three kids at their homework and go to HCE's pub, where somebody is singing "The Ballad of the Sockerson Boy." (371.30–32) "From Dancingtree till Suttonstone There's lads no lie would filch a crown To mull their sack and brew their tay With wather parted from the say." Brunton the butler finds himself in the company of Macbeth, Richard III and King Arthur's foster brother. The lad tried to filch the ancient crown. He followed the route from the elm tree to a certain stone (Suttonstone). An image of Stuart days is evoked by "mull their sack." But more to the point is the linen sack in which Brunton put the Stuart crown. The sack was subsequently thrown into the mere, suggesting that American innovation, the tea bag (brew their tay).

The association of tea with a treasure thrown into the water recalls the Agra treasure of *The Sign of the Four*. America, tea and sea water suggest the Boston Tea Party. And so we return to the letter from Boston.

(94.20–22) "Now tell me, tell me, tell me then!

What was it?
A.................!
?...............O!

ALP's letter has been interpreted by Sherlock Holmes in terms of the chart of the Agra treasure and of the cipher message in *The Valley of Fear*. Now we see that it also applies to the Musgrave Ritual, a series of catechetical questions (tell me, tell me, tell me). The first question: "Whose was it?"

Chapter 12

The Stock-Broker's Clerk

Allusions to this case are concentrated very clearly on (511–35). The great detective is first detected as Sigerson, but later he assumes his own formidable identity—one of the two cases in *FW* in which Sherlock Holmes is overtly named. It might be mentioned that the plot of *The Stock-Broker's Clerk* is one of the stupidest ever conceived by the criminal (or auctorial) mind.

A newly hired clerk, Hall Pycroft, was lured away from a stockbroker's office so that a thief could assume his identity. Pycroft, who expected to start on a new job shortly, was visited by a Mr. Arthur Pinner, who offered Pycroft another position at more than twice the expected salary. While Pycroft was decoyed to Birmingham, his name and place in the London stockbroker's office were assumed by Arthur Pinner's brother, Harry. Meanwhile Arthur was impersonating brother Harry in the dummy office set up in Birmingham. Pycroft described Arthur Pinner as "dark-haired, dark-eyed, black-bearded." As the false Harry, he "had the same figure and voice, but he was clean-shaven and his hair was lighter."

The impersonation failed a few days later when Pycroft noticed that the man who called himself Harry had a gold filling in a front tooth, identical with that observed in the mouth of Arthur. "When I put that with the voice and figure being the same and the only things altered which might be changed by a razor or a wig, I could not doubt that it was the same man," explained Pycroft to Sherlock Holmes, on a quick trip to London. Whereupon Pycroft returned to Birmingham accompanied by Holmes and Watson in the guise of two more job seekers.

(511.17–20) "—That perkumiary pond is beyawned my pinnigay pretonsions …

"—You are suckersome! But this all, as airs said to oska."

Pycroft was overwhelmed at the offer of £500 a year from Pinner (pinnigay), who implied that Pycroft would be a sucker to accept less in London. Using the alias "Harris" in Birmingham, Holmes asked Pinner for a job as an accountant. Adaline Glasheen has idetfied Frank Harris and Oscar Wilde in "airs said to osca." So Holmes is brought into this passage both as Sigerson (suckersome) and as Harris (airs).

(533.29–31) "Michael Engels is your man. Let Michael relay Sutton and tell you people here who have the phoney habit (it was remarketable)." Here is a suggestion of one man replacing another (as in a relay race) for deceptive purposes (phoney) involving the stock market (it was remarketable). Here also may be Willie "the Actor" Sutton, a notorious American robber and disguise artist, who in 1930 participated in a jewel robbery impersonating a Western Union messenger, who relayed messages (relay Sutton). In subsequent crimes in the early thirties Sutton impersonated a policeman, a postman, a bank guard and a window washer.[1]

The archangel Michael (Michael Engels) "durst not bring against [Satan-Sutton] a railing accusation, but said, The Lord rebuke thee" (Jude IX). Similarly Hall Pycroft made no accusation against Pinner, but turned the problem over to Sherlock Holmes. Coincidently, a bank robber named Sutton, under the assumed name of Blessington, was a murder victim in another Sherlockian case, *The Resident Patient*. To add to the complexity, relevant or not, the real name of the Pinner brothers in *The Stock-Broker's Clerk* turned out to be Beddington.

(533.33–36) "Pimpin's Ornery forninehalf. Shaun Shemsen saywhen saywhen. Holmstock unsteaden. Livpoomark lloyrge hoggs one four tupps noying." Pinner induced Pycroft to rattle off a string of stock market quotations to see whether he had "kept in touch with the market." Joyce's "Holmstock unsteaden" may be a critical comment on the small contribution made by Holmes to the solution of this case. He just happened to be around at the time.

(534.3–36) The entire page is dotted with nonsequential allusions to the case. We shall try to consider them in chronological order. (534.11–12) "And I contango can take off ... quoting here in Pynix Park." The *Oxford English Dictionary* defines: "Contango, *Stock Exchange*, the percentage which a buyer of stock pays to the seller to delay transfer." Pinner gave Pycroft £100 in spot cash to delay his transfer to the new job. (534.5) "His jew placator." Pycroft remarked that Pinner had "a touch of the sheeny about his nose." And he was eager to placate Pycroft. (534.8) "Colt's tooth!" The gold tooth Pycroft "saw with a thrill."

(534.20–21) "He is cunvessor to Saunter's Nocelettres and the Poe's Toffee's Directory in his pisness." In order to keep Pycroft busy in Birmingham, Pinner assigned him the task of copying the names and addresses of hardware dealers out of the Paris city directory. (534.29–30) "He was leaving out of my double inns while he was all teppling over my single ixits." Subtle, complex and amusing. Pycroft speaking about Harry Pinner in London: He was living as my double while he was tampering and dabbling with my double-entry bookkeeping (double inns ... single ixits).

(534.31–535.1) "Sherlook is lorking for him. Allare beltspanners ... Hanging Tower! ... Flap, my Larrybird! Dangle my highflyer! Jiggety jig my jackadandyline!" Holmes and Watson were introduced to Arthur Pinner in Birmingham as job applicants. However Pinner was emotionally distraught. He had just read a newspaper account of the failure of the robbery attempt in London and the arrest of his brother for murder. In despair, Pinner excused himself and retired to an inner room, where he attempted suicide by hanging himself in his braces (beltspanners).

(534.3) "Tiktak. Tikkak." Pinner's air-dancing feet were kicking at the door. "Again and much louder came the rat-tat-tat ... the clatter of his heels against the door made the noise." Holmes and Watson rushed into the other room and released the noose, saving Pinner for prison.

Page 534 is especially noteworthy as an example of Joyce's technique in weaving the dream motif into *FW*. The "Tikkak" noise occurs at the top of the page, when logically it should occur at the bottom. This is because the "Tikkak" is more than Pinner's kick. It is also the sound of a twig or an ivy leaf wind-blown against the window, disturbing the sleep of the dreamer. The noise recurs in many different contexts throughout *FW*.

(535.1) "Let me never see his waddphez again!" The revived Pinner's face was "clay-coloured" (waddphezz). "He did not turn pale. He was pale," said Holmes.

(535.26–27) "—Old Whitehowth he is speaking again. Ope Eustace tube! Pity poor whiteoath! Dear gone mummeries, goby!" Pinner explained his suicide attempt by referring to the newspaper story. " 'The paper!' croaked a voice behind us. The man was sitting up, blanched and ghastly... and hands which rubbed nervously at the broad red band which still encircled his throat" (Ope Eustace tube).

There is a Mamafesta title for this case: (106.17–19) "*It was Me Egged Him on to The Stork Exchange and Lent my Dutiful Face to His Customs.*"

Joyce's special interest in this story is readily understood. There are multiple impersonations; everybody is somebody else, even Watson. And according to Frank Budgen, Joyce "regarded the English interest in crime in the shape of the detective story as exceptionally ludicrous."[2] It would be difficult to imagine anything more ludicrous than the maladroit scheme of the Pinner brothers. Neither Holmes nor even the Scotland Yard bunglers were needed. A certain "Sergeant Tuson of the City police" picked up the pieces. The concept of crime as comic also might explain the possible inclusion of the amusing exploits of Willie "the Actor" Sutton.

NOTES

1. Another notorious American criminal is mentioned in *FW:* (602.24) "Dutch Shulds, perhumps."

2. Frank Budgen, *James Joyce and the Making of* Ulysses (Oxford: Oxford University Press, 1972), 191.

Chapter 13

The Adventure of the Norwood Builder

A vindictive builder, Jonas Oldacre, sought long-deferred revenge for a broken engagement.[1] He made a will leaving his property to his ex-fiancée's son, John Hector MacFarlane. Oldacre then staged a fake murder of himself, with falsified evidence pointing to MacFarlane, and disappeared, hiding in a secret room in his own house. Brief isolated allusions to the false evidence of the murder appear in *FW*. These include the following elements:

- A pair of Oldacre's trousers burned in a woodpile.
- Some charred metal buttons from the trousers.
- An animal body of some kind burned with the trousers.
- A bloody thumb print planted on a wall.

Although only two of the numerous phoenix allusions in *FW* seem to have relevance to Oldacre, it should be noted that he enacted the role in rising alive from his own ashes. The police had assumed that Oldacre's corpse was burned in the woodpile.

(62.6–11) "Expiating manslaughter and reberthing in remarriement out of dead seekness to devine previdence, (if you are looking for the bilder deep your ear on the movietone!) to league his lot, palm and patte, with a papishee. For mine qvinne I thee giftake and bind my hosenband I thee halter." Holmes forced the builder to come out of hiding by leading shouts of "Fire!" in the corridor of the house. This was the tone that moved Oldacre (movietone). James Quin (qvinne) was an eighteenth-century Irish actor who was convicted of manslaughter. Oldacre bequeathed his fortune (league his lot) to MacFarlane as legatee. Oldacre's burned trousers (*Hosen*—

German) constituted the *corpus delicti* that would put MacFarlane's neck in a halter (bind my hosenband I thee halter). And it was his mother's choice of a husband (remarriement) that motivated the frame-up.

(100.2–3) "Shall their hope then be silent or Macfarlane lack of lamentation?" The framed MacFarlane hoped to get help from Sherlock Holmes. " Mr. Holmes, I am the unhappy John Hector MacFarlane.' "

(455.23) "Hyam Hyam's in the chair." The charred (chair) trouser buttons bore the name of Oldacre's tailor, "Hyams." The French word *chair* means "flesh," and when Oldacre prepared the fake crematory pyre he included the carcass of an animal so that "all the firemen smelled the burned flesh." (453.15–16) "While Old Clo goes through the wood with Shep togather." Holmes asked the captured Oldacre, "By the way, what was it you put into the wood-pile besides your old trousers [Old Clo]? A dead dog [Shep], or rabbits, or what?"

The Norwood Builder appears again on a page naming Doyle and including allusions to *Silver Blaze* previously noted. This is consistent since both Oldacre and the horse, Silver Blaze, were resurrected by Holmes. (322.14–23) "Chorus: With his coat so graye. And his pounds that he pawned from the burning ... from spark to phoenish. ... And they peered him beheld on the pyre." The parody of the fox-hunting song "John Peel" is relevant. "His 'View Halloo!' would awaken the dead,/ And the fox from his lair in the morning." The foxy Oldacre was awakened from the dead by a chorus of shouts and driven from his lair. Oldacre burned his pants but not his coat. And before he lit the pyre he took care that all his money was transferred to a secret bank account in the name of a mythical "Mr. Cornelius." (98.8–10) "And was even now occupying, under an islamitic newhame in his seventh generation, a physical body Cornelius Magrath's (badoldkarakter)." BAD OLD AK ER.

(111.20–22) "The stain, and that a teastain (the overcautelousness of the masterbilker here, as usual, signing the page away), marked it off on the spout of the moment as a genuine relique." The passage will be recognized as part of ALP's Mamafesta, or the letter from Boston. In this context the stain is a bloody thumbprint (T-stain) which Oldacre (the masterbilker) planted on the wall of his house as evidence against MacFarlane. The print was obtained by having MacFarlane press his thumb against sealing wax to seal up a legal document (signing the page away). The thumbprint provides another demonstration of Holmes's ability to decipher the cryptic letter. He immediately recognized that the evidence was false. The *Oxford English Dictionary* defines: "*Cautelousness, Obs* ... craftiness." Jonas Oldacre was undeniably a crafty schemer, as was his Norwegian colleague, Halvard Solness, Henrik Ibsen's *Masterbuilder*. And it might be added that both "masterbilkers" ended up by bilking themselves.

(280.21–23) "With best from cinder Christinette if prints chumming, can be when desires Soldi, for asamples." Oldacre was the cinder Christ (phoenix), who desired a sample of his chum's thumbprint. Perhaps "Soldi" combines Oldacre with the other master builder, Solness. Also *soldi* (Italian—pennies, small change). Since Oldacre had transferred all of his assets to "Mr. Cornelius," MacFarlane could have inherited nothing of value. (280, left margin) "*How matches metrooseers*?" Oldacre put a match to his trousers.

The bloody thumbprint appears again. (608.1–11) "It is a mere mienerism of this vague of visibilities, mark you, as accorded to by moisturologist of the Brehons Assorceration for the advauncement of scayence ... surprised in an indecorous position by the Sigurd Sigerson Sphygmomanometer Society for bledprusshers." Both a spiritualistic seance and science are combined in "scayence." Of course we recognize Holmes as Sigerson. A sphygmomanometer is the pneumatic cuff used by physicians to measure blood pressure. The false thumbprint was created with blood, pressure and wax.

The preceding page includes an allusion to the device used by Holmes in driving Oldacre from his hiding place and to Oldacre's appearance and discomfiture. The device involved burning some smoky wet straw in the corridor followed by shouts of "Fire!"

(607.18–35) "(attempted by the admirable Captive Bunting and Loftonant-Cornel Blaire) will processingly show up above Tumplen Bar whereupont he was much jubilated by Boergemester ... looking most plusssed with (exhib 39) a clout capped sunbubble anaccanponied from his bequined torse. ... Grand old Manbutton." "Captive Bunting" is MacFarlane who, in a sense, was wrapped up in a rabbit skin—the pair of rabbits burned in the woodpile. The loft tenant is Plainly Oldacre. The heads of executed criminals were at one time exhibited over Temple Bar in London. "Boergemester" is Ibsen's *Masterbuilder* (*Bygmester*—Norwegian). The "clout" refers

(*FW* 608.1–11) It is a mere mienerism of this vague of visibilities, mark you, as accorded to by moisturologist of the Brehons Assorceration for the advauncement of scayence . . . surprised in an indecorous position by the Sigurd Sigerson Sphygmomanometer Society for bledprusshers.

Sherlock Holmes, with handprint added by William Jenkins. From *Conan Doyles' Best Books* (New York: P. F. Collier and Son, n.d.), frontispiece.

both to the trousers and to the cloud of smoke above the flame (sunbubble) which was unaccompanied by his murdered (bequined, as by James Quin) body.

(210.7–8) "A cough and a rattle and wildrose cheeks for poor Piccolina Petite MacFarlane." Glasheen suggests that "Piccolina" refers to Picciola, a story about a lonely prisoner who grew a little flower in his cell.[2] Therefore, as pure conjecture: MacFarlane was released from prison with an embrrassed cough from Lestrade, a rattle, as the cell door was unlocked, and rosy cheeks replacing prison pallor.

An ALP Mamafesta title that applies with equal relevance to *Silver Blaze*: (105.28–29) "*How to Pull a Good Horuscoup even when Oldsire is Dead to the World.*"

NOTES

1. *The Adventure of the Norwood Builder* was first published in *The Strand* magazine, November 1903. The previous issue of *The Strand,* October 1903, carried *The Adventure of the Empty House,* wherein Homes related to Watson the details of his duel with Professor Moriarty at Reichenbach Falls. (453.4) "fighting your biddy moriarty duels."

2. This recalls Tom Sawyer's demand that the captive Jim grow a mullen stalk in his cabin: "And don't call it mullen, call it Pitchiola—that's its right name when it's in prison."

Chapter 14

Silver Blaze

This tale of a stolen, disguised and resurrected racehorse does not figure largely in *FW*. Sherlock Holmes appears fleetingly as part of the Norwegian captain complex. However, Joyce seems to have used some allusions for political comment directed at Doyle, who is specifically named. Appropriately, the sporting and political discussion is heard at the bar in HCE's pub.

(322.1–4) Kersse the tailor, dressed as a seaman, comes into the pub, back from the Baldoyle racetrack, "his old Conan over his top gallant shouldier." (322.16–20) "Who did you do at doyle today, my horsey dorksey gentryman. ... Kersse stood them the whole kourse of training how the whole blazy raze acurraghed ... from spark to phoenish." At the "phoenish" of the race, Silver Blaze, who had been given up for lost, was resurrected and revealed as the winner. "You have only to wash his face and his leg in spirits of wine, and you will find that he is the same old Silver Blaze as ever," explained Holmes.

(322.25–26) "—Same capman no nothing horces two feller he feller go where." As the Norwegian captain, Holmes would wear a sailor's cap, similar to Kersse's (same capman). However, he was wearing his familiar deerstalker when, accompanied by Watson (two feller), he found the missing horse by following its tracks (he feller go where).

(328.27) Somebody in the pub mentioned a song entitled "The Steeplepoy's Revanger." The drugged stable boy was amply revenged by Silver Blaze, who killed the culprit with a kick.

The horse race, now called the world renowned Caerholme Event, is described over the television. (342.6–9) "*Bawldawl the curse, baledale the day! And the frocks of shick sheeples in their shummering insamples! You see: ... a middinest from the Casabianca.*" In order to learn the technique for laming Silver Blaze, the dishonest trainer, Straker, practised on a flock of sheep (insamples). He kept an expensive mistress, a fact Sherlock Holmes learned from a milliner's bill (French, *midinette*—middinest).

(323.26) "(Riland's in peril!) with its doomed crack of the old damn ukonnen." The stable at King's Pyland (Riland) was indeed in peril with the favored Silver Blaze missing. But Ireland was also in peril according to Doyle, who is identified with the U.K. (ukonnen). In 1886 Doyle is known to have written, "Ireland is a huge suppuration which will go on suppurating until it bursts."[1]

(341.20–21) "*The worldrenownced Caerholme Event has been being given by* The Irish Race." The Welsh word caer means "castle," and to Dubliners "the castle" meant Dublin Castle, the seat of British rule and headquarters for the Royal Irish Constabulary.[2] That the "Caerholme Event" is a gift of "The Irish Race" seems to be an ironic reference to Doyle's ancestry, his political Unionism and his creation of Sherlock Holmes, the great prop of British law and order.

Silver Blaze "is from the Somomy stock and holds as brilliant a record as his famous ancestor ... he was the first favorite for the Wessex Cup." The pedigree of the resurrected racehorse and the name of the Wessex Cup may have inspired a Mamafesta title: (105.28–29) "*How to Pull a Good Horuscoup even when Oldsire is Dead to the World.*"

NOTES

1. John Dickson Carr, *The Life of Sir Arthur Conan Doyle* (New York: Harper and Brothers, 1949), 48.

2. Cf. (*U* 163): "All the time drawing secret service pay from the castle."

Chapter 15

The Adventure of the Illustrious Client

The case of a man whose face was changed permanently and against his will was that of Baron Adelbert Gruner, womanizer, murderer and expert on Chinese pottery. The concentration on two pages in *FW* of these very clear allusions demonstrates again a most important common feature of the Sherlock Holmes stories used by Joyce. Almost without exception there is an element of changed identity. Faces change, aliases are employed, disguises are assumed. In this case even Watson attempts a deceptive impersonation.

In *FW* the story becomes part of a playlet entitled (219.18–20) "*The Mime of Mick, Nick and the Maggies*, adopted from the Balleymooney Bloodridden Murther by Bluechin Blackdillain." Holmes is cast in the role of (221.6–10) SAUNDERSON ... unconcerned in the mystery." As the archangel Michael (Mick) is the agent of God, than whom no client could be more illustrious, Holmes was the agent of King Edward VII. His opponent (Old Nick) was Baron Adelbert Gruner, a satanic wife-murderer (Bluechin Blackdillain equals Bluebeard and Othello). The case was not a mystery (unconcerned in the mystery) but rather a struggle to save the beautiful and accomplished Violet de Merville from the baron. Having murdered his previous wife, Gruner had become engaged to marry Miss de Merville (220.6–10), "a bewitching blonde ... who is being fatally fascinated."

The contest reached a climax when Holmes entered Gruner's house accompanied by Kitty Winter, the baron's discarded mistress. She helped Holmes find written evidence of Gruner's criminal past, and then took physical revenge by emptying a vial of vitriol, sulfuric acid, in Gruner's face.

Joyce alludes repeatedly to the scene wherein Gruner rolled on the floor in agony after receiving the acid. Watson described Gruner's damaged eyes as "white and glazed ... dead-fish eyes." Joyce says "whipping his eyesoult ... poligone eyes ... blinks you blank.... In the lost of the gleamens ... eyes whiteopen ... spittyful eyes ... lavabad eyes ... off his fleshskin."

Joyce himself was nearly blind in 1930 after many operations for cataracts, which explains his marked empathy for the blinded Gruner. Richard Ellmann's biography records Joyce's interest in other people with eye trouble at this time, and then notes that Joyce began work on the "Mime" chapter shortly after the tenth operation on his eyes.[1]

Page 240 includes numerous allusions to *The Illustrious Client.* (240.5–6) "But low, boys, low, he rises shrivering, with his spittyful eyes and his whoozebecome woice." The baron had received a splash of acid fair in the face. "One eye was already white and glazed. The other was red and inflamed." (240.11–12) "Himserf, munchaowl, born of thug tribe into brood blackmail." Gruner, like another German baron, Munchhausen, was a most accomplished liar, and a most unamusing Till Eulenspiegel (munchaowl). He had a typical blackmailer's personality, although he was not known to be guilty of that specific crime. (240.13) "He, by bletchendmacht of the golls." As Watson said, "one eye was already white" (bletchendmacht). Both blandishment and the bleeding of girls are also suggested. (240.14–16) "He, self sufficiencer, eggscumuddher-in-chaff sporticolorissimo, what though the duthsthrows in his lavabad eyes." A piece of "real egg-shell pottery of the Ming dynasty" (eggscumuddher) figured in the case. It was "of the most beautiful deep-blue color" (sporticolorissimo—as an Oxford "blue"). Watson administered first aid to Gruner. "I bathed his face in oil" (lavabad eyes). (240.17) "Good savours queen with the stem of swuith Aftreck! Fit for king of Zundas." Gruner's house "had been built by a South African gold king." (240.19–25) "No more throw acids, face all loveabilities ... weedhearted boy of potter and mudder ... Teufleuf man he strip him all mussymussy calico." The thrown acid resulted in a face change for Gruner. And for his part, Sherlock Holmes also donned an involuntary disguise. He appeared on the scene, "his head girt with bloody bandages." Holmes had been badly beaten up, but he was tough and still alive (Teufleuf)—and still a disciple of Professor Teufelsdröckh, the philosopher of Carlyle's *Sartor Resartus*.

Following these almost certain references on page 240, we find one slightly less certain on the facing page. (241.14) "Mistress Mereshame, of cupric tresses." This is probably Kitty Winter, the acid thrower, who led a life of shame. Watson described her as "flame-like," so it is presumed she had red hair. An association between eye damage and a flame is found on an earlier page. (232.2–7) "For the mauwe that blinks you blank is mostly Carbo ... with a pure flame and a true flame and a flame all toogasser, soot. The worst is over ... In the lost of the gleamens." As a discarded mistress, Kitty Winter was Gruner's "old flame." Vitriol, sulfuric acid, is used in making dyestuffs and other carbon compounds (mauve—Carbo). Also "mauwe" perhaps for Violet de Merville. And "cupric" may mean more than copper-colored hair. Cupric sulfate is also called blue vitriol. This compound is strongly irritant to the skin, but not immediately corrosive like sulfuric acid.

(222.26–27) "He was sbuffing and sputing, tussing like anisine, whipping his eyesoult and gnatsching his teats." When the vitriol was thrown in his face, "the Baron uttered a horrible cry ... he fell upon the carpet, rolling and writhing ... 'It was that hell-cat, Kitty Winter,' he cried" (whipping his eyesoult—Isolde).

(229.29–32) "And reading off his fleshskin ... a most moraculous jeermyhead sindbook for all the peoples." Kitty Winter told Holmes: "Its a book he has—a brown leather book with a lock. ... This man collects women and takes pride in his collection as some men collect moths or butterflies. He had it all in that book. Snapshot photographs, names, details.... It was a beastly book" (sindbook).

(231.29–31) "He threwed his fit up to his aers, rolled his poligone eyes, snivelled from his snose and blew the guff." (234.7–9) "With eyes whiteopen ... Of all the green heroes ... the whitemost" (green hero—Gruner).

NOTE

1. Richard Ellmann, *James Joyce* (New York: Oxford University Press, 1959), 634–41.

Chapter 16

Footprints—More Designs on the Corse

The first Sherlock Holmes story was *A Study in Scarlet*, published in 1887. Perhaps James Joyce never read it. At any rate, there seem to be no allusions to it in *FW*. Next to *The Sign of the Four*, Joyce seems to have been most interested in the first six stories appearing in *The Return of Sherlock Holmes*. All of these were published first in *The Strand* magazine from September 1903 to March 1904. In January 1904 Joyce began to write *Stephen Hero*, which later would be revised as *A Portrait of the Artist as a Young Man*.[1] The influence of Doyle's early novel *The Stark-Munro Letters* on *Stephen Hero* and *Ulysses*, wherein *Stark-Munro* is acknowledged as an overdue library book, has been shown.

For the sake of complete documentation, the apparent inclusion in *FW* of additional adventures from the Holmes saga is given below. In some cases these allusions are so faint as to be mere fragments of whispers. Others seem very clear, but also very short. In any event, it must be conceded that their presence remains very much an open question.

THE ADVENTURE OF THE SPECKLED BAND

If this adventure is indeed in *FW*, it is evoked primarily by the atmosphere of pages 572–78. HCE's incestuous impulse toward his sleeping daughter is of some relevance. So is the legal discussion wherein judges, jurors and a witness all seem to be named "Doyle."

The Holmes story involves the attempted murder by Dr. Grimesby Roylott of his stepdaughter to prevent her marriage.

Roylott, who had already murdered one stepdaughter for the same reason, had been living on the income of the surviving sister. Under the terms of their dead mother's will, all property would revert to the girls in the event of marriage.

(576.4–7) "Mamy's mancipium act did not apply and therefore held supremely that, as no property in law can exist in a corpse, (Hal Kilbride *v* Una Bellina) Pepigi's pact was pure piffle (loud laughter) and Wharrem would whistle for the rhino." Roylott's murder method was to introduce a venomous snake into the bed of his sleeping stepdaughter. He summoned the snake by whistling.

(576.12–13) "—Lest he forewaken.

"—Hide ourselves."

Holmes and Watson hid themselves in the stepdaughter's bedroom and awaited the murder attempt.

(576.27–32) "Bogy Bobow with his cunnyngnest couchmare, Big Maester Finnykin ... down their laddercase of nightwatch service and bring them at suntime flush with the nethermost gangrung of their stepchildren." *Conan* Doyle may be concealed here (cunnyn). To effect his plan Roylott had part of the house rebuilt (Master Builder—Big Maester). The snake had been trained to climb down a bellpull (laddercase of nightwatch service) which hung directly over the pillow.

(578.3–8) "This mitryman, some king of the yeast in his chrismy greyed brunzewig. ... Relics of pharrer and livite! ... He has only his hedcosycasket on and his woollsey shirtplisse with peascod doublet, and also his feet wear doubled." Watson described Roylott's appearance after the snake had turned on him. "Dr. Grimesby Roylott, clad in a long grey dressing gown, his bare ankles protruding beneath, and his feet thrust into red heelless Turkish slippers. ... Round his brow he had a peculiar yellow band, with brownish speckles, which seemed to be bound tightly round his head." The yellow band "with brownish speckles" (brunzewig) which crowned Dr. Roylott (king of the yeast) was, of course, the snake. Joyce may refer to the snake in "Relics of pharrer and livite!" This suggests Aaron's rod, turned into a serpent to impress pharaoh. The Levites were the servants of the priests, the sons of Aaron.

THE CROOKED MAN

Colonel James Barclay, commander of an Irish regiment, was found, apparently murdered, in his home at Aldershot. The colonel's lady had been attending a church meeting with a friend, who related an incident that occurred on the way home: "We were returning from the Watt Street Mission, about a quarter to nine o'clock. On our way we had to pass through Hudson Street. ... There is only one lamp ... and as we approached this lamp I saw a man coming towards us with his back very bent and something like a box slung over one of his shoulders. He appeared to be deformed ... . We were passing him when he raised his face and screamed out in a dreadful voice, 'My God, it's Nancy!' "

(62.27–33) "It was after the show at Wednesbury that one tall man, humping a suspicious parcel, when returning late amid a dense particular on his home way ... by the old spot, Roy's Corner, had a barkiss revolver placed to his faced with the words: you're shot major by an unknowable assailant (masked) against whom he had been jealous over, Lotta Crabtree or Pomona Evlyn."

It was learned that Colonel Barclay had indeed been jealous of the crooked stranger, Henry Wood, when they had served in the same regiment in bygone years. Barclay had betrayed Wood, causing him to be captured by the enemy during the Sepoy Mutiny. The mistreatment Wood received during his long captivity caused his deformity. When Wood, back in England, broke into the Barclay home and confronted his betrayer, the colonel died of heart failure. "The bare sight of me was like a bullet through his guilty heart," explained Wood.

(67.11–15) "Long Lally Tobkids, the special, sporting a fine breast of medals, and a conscientious scripturereader to boot in the brick and tin choorch round the coroner, swore like a Norewheeszian tailliur ... that he was up against a right querrshnorrt of a mand." This passage seems to suggest Sherlock Holmes as Lally, a veteran soldier (fine breast of medals) meeting a queer sort of man returning from the Watt Street Mission (the brick and tin choorch).

THE ADVENTURE OF THE SOLITARY CYCLIST

This story was published in *The Strand* in January 1904, a month after *The Dancing Men* and a month before *The Priory School.*

(115.13–20) "Some softnosed peruser might mayhem take it up erogenously as the usual case of spoons, *prostituta* in herba plus dinky pinks deliberatively summersaulting off her bisexycle, at the main entrance of curate's perpetual soutane suit with her one to see and awoh! who picks her up as gingerly as any balmbearer would to feel whereupon the virgin was most hurt and nicely asking: whyre have you been so grace a mauling and where were you chaste me child."

Miss Violet Smith, an attractive music teacher, had many admirers, including an unknown pursuer (peruser) who regularly chased (chaste) her across the heath (herba). Holmes rescued her after an abduction (mauling) just as a forced marriage was about to be performed by a bogus cleric.

THE ADVENTURE OF WISTERIA LODGE

The case begins with an account of "the singular experience of Mr. John Scott Eccles." Invited to spend the night in a Latin American household, Mr. Eccles awoke in the morning to find himself alone in the house.

(514.9–10) "—Schottenly there was a hellfire club kicked out through the wasistas of Therewhere." Wisteria (wasistas) Lodge was in Oxshott, Surrey. "Schottenly" combines Oxshott with Mr. Eccles given name, Scott. The mulatto cook was a voodoo worshiper who practised "unclean" sacrificial rites, recalling the Hell Fire Club at Medmenham Abbey near Henley on Thames where, in 1750, devil worshipers celebrated the Black Mass.[2]

(514.19) "—Ninny there is no hay in Eccles's hostel," Eccles found nobody in the house the next morning. In the Spanish of his Latin American host, *no hay ninguno*.

(567.27) "Me Eccls! What cats' killings over all!" Mr. Eccles, "the very type of conventional British respectability," was shocked to find himself involved in a murder committed by the fugitive ex-dictator Murillo, "The Tiger of San Pedro," and his secretary, Lopez, also described as "cat-like."

Incidentally, "no hay in Eccles hostel" also includes the "Ithaca" episode in *Ulysses*. Leopold Bloom invited Stephen Dedalus to spend the night in his house in Eccles Street, Dublin. Stephen declined.

THE ADVENTURE OF THE DEVIL'S FOOT

(193.4–18) "Don't tell me, Leon of the fold, that you are not a loanshark! Lookup, old sooty be advised by mux and take your medicine. The Good Doctor mulled it. Mix it twice before repastures and powder three times a day. ... If the baryshnyas got a twitter of it they'd tell the housetops and then all Cadbury would go crackers. ... I had it from Lamppost Shaw. And he had it from the Mullah."

Dr. Leon Sterndale, an African explorer, returned to England with a quantity of powdered root (he had it from the Mullah) which emitted a poisonous smoke when burned (sooty). Two people were killed and two rendered insane (crackers) by the powder. The local vicar cried, "My poor parish [parishioners—barishnyas] is devil-ridden!" Holmes retrieved some of the unburned powder from the lamp.

THE PROBLEM OF THOR BRIDGE

Watson begins his narration by mentioning three unpublished cases of Sherlock Holmes: "Among these unfinished tales is that of Mr. James Phillimore, who, stepping back into his own house to get his umbrella, was never more seen in this world." Among the names of the twelve Morphios in the "Riddles" chapter of *FW* are: (142.28) "Philly, Jamesy Mor." One of the twelve apostles of Christ was named Philip, and two were named James. Unlike James the Greater (Jamesy Mor), but like James Phillimore, James the Less (or the Little) is little more than a name.

NOTES

1. Richard Ellmann, *James Joyce* (New York, Oxford University Press, 1959), 149.
2. Henry Blyth, *The Rakes* (New York: Dial Press, 1971), 92.

Chapter 17

Motif and Leitmotif (Book I, Chapters 1–8)

It has seemed preferable to organize this study of Sherlock Holmes in *FW* along horizontal (Sherlockian) rather than vertical (Joycean) lines. By taking allusions out of sequence as they occur in *FW*, and grouping them roughly in sequence with a particular Holmes story, it has been possible to avoid much repetitious explanation and the discussion of too many things at once.

In many cases however, horizontal organization has resulted in loss of the full effect of the Sherlock Holmes motif proper, which is developed in some passages of *FW* through allusions to several different stories on the same page.

FW is organized into seventeen chapters divided among four books. Joyce did not bestow titles on any of the divisions of his completed work, and the chapters are not even numbered. However, some commentators have found it convenient to use the ad hoc titles Joyce gave to a few of the chapters, which were published earlier and separately. For the chapters untitled by Joyce, these commentators have taken the pardonable liberty of inventing titles that may be helpfully descriptive.

It would be neither enlightening nor practical to attempt a complete chapter-by-chapter analysis of the Sherlockian allusions in *FW*. However, a brief discussion of some of them may be helpful in showing how the specific cases relate to the themes of individual chapters. At least the discussion should not add to the confusion. Non-Sherlockian interpretations will be given wherever: (a) they add meaning to the Holmes allusions; (b) they are original as far as I know; and (c) whim dictates.

It should be emphasized that the chapter analyses which follow are not intended to summarize all the important elements of each chapter. They are merely an attempt to set at least part of a scene. Readers who wish to broaden their understanding of *FW* beyond the scope of this work should turn to the excellent guides by Campbell and Robinson and by Tindall.[1]

CHAPTER 1. THE FALL (PP. 3–29)

The ballad of Finnegan's great fall and Here Comes Everybody, including Sherlock Holmes. The greatest detective of them all is depicted very early on, baring his arm for a shot of cocaine as in *The Sign of the Four.* (5.5) "Of the first was he to bare arms." Holmes is honored by association with the first man to fall from grace, Adam, and the association comes by way of the greatest masterpiece in English literature, *Hamlet*, V, 1:

> FIRST CLOWN. ...There is no ancient gentlemen but gardeners, ditchers, and gravemakers; they hold up Adam's profession.
> SECOND CLOWN. Was he a gentleman?
> FIRST CLOWN. He was the first that ever bore arms.

We next find Holmes named as (15.35) "Comestipple Sacksoun" and on the next page (16.33–34) "Cedric Silkyshag ... bar, old grilsy growlsy," a grizzly bear. These identifications occur in the Mutt and Jute episode, which names Doyle, relates to *The Hound of the Baskervilles* and hints at other aspects of Holmes. He is a honey-loving bear and bee keeper; an upholder of British law, hence an imperialist and Saxon invader; a disguise specialist; a cryptographer who reads (18.17) "this claybook" and whose own saga is included therein; a drug addict and a heavy smoker.

On pages 21–23 comes the story of the prankquean and Jarl van Hoother, reflecting the plot of *The Priory School* and concluding with (23.11) "a sweet unclose to the Narwhealian captol," Holmes as the Norwegian captain, derived from "Black Peter".

(25.5) "Poppypap's a passport out" is the first reference to *The Final Problem*, showing Holmes fleeing England disguised as an old Italian priest. (26.2–4) "Hopkins and Hopkins" begins a short passage concerning Stanley Hopkins and John Hopley Neligan from *Black Peter*, and (26.15–22) includes the "headboddylwatcher" cryptogram and other elements from *The Dancing Men*.

CHAPTER 2. THE BALLAD OF PERSSE O'REILLY (PP. 30–47)

The mysterious crime of HCE—original sin. Holmes cannot solve the case because he is guilty also and cannot incriminate himself. This is demonstrated by allusions to his most notable failure, *A Scandal in Bohemia*, which runs through (32.5–35). Holmes not only is capable of error, but he responds to female flesh and the female presence—Irene Adler. "To Sherlock Holmes she is always *the* woman."

CHAPTER 3. TESTIMONY AND PROMISED PARDON (PP. 48–74)

The testimony of certain witnesses suggests that HCE, though guilty, was provoked. Therefore he will be pardoned eventually. Since the crime was original sin, a pardon means resurrection from death. Holmes allusions carry out the resurrection theme, including (57.20–5B.24) *The Empty House*; (62.6–11) *The Norwood Builder*, who emulated the phoenix in rising from the ashes of his own body; and (62.27–35) *The Crooked Man*, a former soldier believed dead in India returned to England. Also noted (67.11) is the first appearance of Holmes as Lally, the name derived from two Indian servants in *The Sign of the Four*.

CHAPTER 4. TRIAL AND VERDICT (PP. 75–103)

The evidence in the trial of HCE as Festy King is so confusing that the verdict is an inconclusive (93.1) "Nolans Brumans." Pages 81–91 include a great many strong allusions to *The Man with the Twisted Lip*, highly relevant since this was also a case of Nolans Brumans. A suspected murderer and his victim were discovered to be one and the same man—Giordano Bruno's unity of opposites. Also, since the supposed murder victim arose from a watery grave in the Thames, it is another case of resurrection.

ALP's letter is introduced as evidence after the verdict is in. Holmes, the great cryptographer, can read it, as was demonstrated by (89.31–90.16) *The Adventure of the Dancing Men.* Holmes as a bear: (94.10–26) "the old hunks on the hill read it to perlection." On this page the letter is the cipher message from *The Valley of Fear* and also the cryptic *Musgrave Ritual.*

CHAPTER 5. THE LETTER FROM BOSTON, MASS. (PP. 104–25)

The four-page (104–7) catalogue of titles for the Mamafesta includes one for the entire Sherlockian canon, which explains the names "Box and Cox" for Watson and Holmes respectively. The catalogue also includes titles for six individual Sherlockian cases.

On (111.8–21) the contents of the letter are revealed and we see that it is the Agra treasure map of *The Sign of the Four* and the bloody thumbprint (T-stain) of *The Norwood Builder.* (124.1–10) The letter from Boston reappears as the Agra treasure chart. It also involves Sherlock Holmes's literary godfather, Dr. Oliver Wendell Holmes, (124.9–10) "Brofesor ath e's Break—fast—table," a well-known man of letters from Boston. Although Doyle never specifically mentioned it, there is strong documentary evidence indicating that the family name of Holmes, the Sage of Boston, was deliberately bestowed on the Sage of Baker Street.[2]

CHAPTER 6. WHODUNIT AND WHAT IS IT? (PP. 126–68)

Twelve riddles are posed by Shem and answered by Shaun. Number 5, the "Help Wanted" ad for a manservant, is discussed at length, but Holmes does not seem to be present. The ad is answered by (141.27) "Pore ole Joe," identified later as (254.24) "old Joe the Java Jane," another detective, Inspector Javert, and Jean Valjean of *Les Misérables.* The long answer to riddle number 11 contains the first overt *FW* mention of (165.30–36) "Shedlock Holmes." The passage includes *The Sign of the Four*, Doyle as a writer and his freeing of Oscar Slater. (165.15–16) "*The Very Picture of a Needlesswoman*" refers to the desperately sought portrait of Irene Adler in *A Scandal in Bohemia.*

CHAPTER 7. SHEM THE PENMAN (PP. 169–195)

Contains very few Holmesian allusions, but these are not inconsistent with a Shem-Sherlock relationship. (180.5–6) "*Deal Little Shemlockup Yellin.*"

CHAPTER 8. ANNA LIVIA PLURABELLE (PP. 196–216)

The Woman who tempted Man to his fall and brought sin to the world is symbolized by the fructifying River Liffey. (200.11–13) "Warbly sangs from over homen: *High hellskirts saw ladies hensmoker lily-hung pigger.*" Holmes used a smoke rocket (hensmoker) to trick the contralto (warbly sangs) Irene Adler into revealing the hiding place of her picture (lily-hung pigger) in *A Scandal in Bohemia*. Gifts from ALP to her children are bestowed on (210.10) "poor Piccolina Petite MacFarlane" in *The Norwood Builder* and on (211.27) "Reuben Redbreast" in *The Priory School*. In the latter cases the crimes committed had a sexual genesis.

NOTES

1. Joseph Campbell and Henry Morton Robinson, *A Skeleton Key to Finnegans Wake* (New York: Viking Press, 1961); William York Tindall, *A Reader's Guide to Finnegans Wake* (New York: Farrar, Strauss and Giroux, 1969).

2. William D. Jenkins, "From a Drop of Water, an Atlantic, a Niagara ..., From a Pebble, the Universe." *Baker Street Journal* 25, no. 3 (September 1975), 166–67.

(*FW* 517.16) They rolled in the ditch together.

The death of Sherlock Holmes. Illustration by Sidney Paget, 1893. From "The Adventure of the Final Problem" in *The Illustrated Sherlock Holmes Treasury* (New York: Avenel Books, 1976), 314.

Chapter 18

Motif and Leitmotif (II, 9–12)

CHAPTER 9. THE MIME OF MICK, NICK AND THE MAGGIES (PP. 219–59)

Holmes is (221.6) "SAUNDERSON (Mr Knut Oelsvinger)," an old knout-swinger and the archangel Michael, defender of the Heavenly Establishment.

A felicitous example of thematic relevance is offered by *The Adventure of the Illustrious Client.* All the allusions seem to occur in this single chapter, and they have been adequately discussed.

Although Holmes is initially identified with Mick-Chuff, he is later importantly identified with Nick-Glugg as well. This is in the passage on page 228 wherein many Irish authors are named. (228.13) "A conansdream" combines *Conan* Doyle with Glugg's dream of "Exile, Silence, Cunning," as employed by Sherlock Holmes in *The Final Problem* and *The Empty House* and by Stephen Dedalus in *A Portrait of the Artist as a Young Man.* Switching identities from Mick to Nick is consistent with the doctrine of Giordano Bruno and his unity of opposites.

(254.24–26) "Old Joe, the Java Jane, older even than Odam Costollo, and we are recurrently meeting em, par Mahun Mesme." Here is another case of the unity of opposites. In *The Man with the Twisted Lip* it was the suspected murderer and his supposed victim. Here, "Java Jane" is both Jean Valjean, the criminal, and Javert, the detective (Mahun Mesme equals same man) from Victor Hugo's *Les Misérables*. But Sherlock Holmes is probably present also. We have already identified him in our *The Hound of the Baskervilles* chapter as (530.21) "Seckerson, magnon," Cro-Magnon man. Now we see him as Java Man (older even than Adam), which explains Joyce's use of the obsolete spelling *mesme* for the French word *même,* meaning "same."

CHAPTER 10. NIGHT LESSONS (PP. 260–308)

The afternoon of play is over, Shem, Shaun and Issy are now doing their homework. They study (306.13–14) "art, literature, politics [ALP], economy, chemistry, humanity [HCE]." That the initials of the father are reversed signals the intent of the twin sons to overthrow him, for the theme of the chapter is revolution and replacement, according to the cyclical theory of human history postulated by Giovanni Battista Vico. And the eventual syntheses of the mutually antithetical twins are an expression of Bruno's unity of opposites. Successful replacement of Here Comes Everybody means that the twins must become Everybody. So they study everything, and the subject matter of the text may reflect anything.

Specific thematic relevance lies in allusions to changed form but unchanging substance. Thus, the first *FW* appearance of Proteus is specifically relevant. No matter what form Proteus assumes, his substance remains constant: (263.16) "not a feature alike and the face the same." Furthermore, he is here (263.1–3) "under the assumed name of Ignotus Loquor," suggesting "ignorant blabbermouth," the antithesis of the omniscient, but stubbornly silent, Proteus. It may be assumed also that the founder of the Jesuits, Ignatius Loyola, was the antithesis of "Ignotus Loquor," the burned (Ignotus equals ignited) heretic, Giordano Bruno. Atherton notes that Bruno was absurdly loquacious and cites Joyce's mockery of a particularly verbose quotation.[1]

The association of Sherlock Holmes with Proteus is apparent here. The left margin alludes to Books IV and VII of *The Odyssey* and very strongly to *The Sign of the Four.* The facing page (161) includes several strong allusions to *The Hound of the Baskervilles*, in the body text, left margin and two footnotes.

The idea of change of form but persistence of substance is carried out pointedly in the structure of the chapter—body text, footnotes and marginalia on both sides. The footnotes, contributed by Issy, are eternally feminine, reflecting her preoccupation with sex and bearing scatterbrained relevance to the text. The war between the twins is fought in the margins.

In the beginning, the right-wing margin notes of Shaun, stuffy and authoritative, are set in uppercase type. The leftist, Shem, jeers in italics. But the middle of page 287 marks the start of a parenthetical passage of five and a half pages devoid of margin notes; and at the top of page 293 we see that Shem has moved to the uppercase right, forcing Shaun to grumble in italics on the left.

It is revolution and counter-revolution—Vico's eternal cycle. The preceding parenthetical passage marks a Viconian *ricorso*, or period of renewal, and the initial Latin lines on page 287 name Giordano Bruno and Giovanni Battista Vico (287.24) "*Jordani et Jambaptistae*." Page 290 includes the Sherlockian case of "Nolans Brumans," *The Man with the Twisted Lip*.

(293, right margin) "WHY MY AS LIKEWISE WHIS HIS." This is the first loud statement by the new top dog, Shem. There is no question mark, but one is certainly implied. Why does the revolution take place on page 293? Literary and historical allusions provide the answer; the end of the *ricorso* and the beginning of the new era are marked by hints of various aspects of rebellion, submission, authority, tyranny and usurpation.

(292.22) "The whole faustian fustion" names Faust, the rebel against God. The picture of change, rebellion and conflict of authority also includes Cardinal Wolsey. (292.F3) "Bussmullah, cried Lord Wolsley, how me Aunty Mag'll row!" At one time Wolsey was bursar (bourse-mullah) of Magdalen (Mag'll) College, Oxford. There was a row over unauthorized use of funds and he resigned. Later he became "boss-mullah" (Arabic, expounder of the law) under Henry VIII, and wielded tyrannical power until overthrown. "Farewell! a long farewell to all my greatness!" (*Henry VIII,* III, 1).

T. S. Eliot seems to be present in Shaun's first counter-revolutionary margin note. This is appropriate, for Eliot led a revolution in English poetry while proclaiming himself "a classicist in literature, a Royalist in politics, and an Anglo-Catholic in religion."[2] And as Tindall and Halper point out, Eliot is consistently identified with Shaun throughout *FW*.[3] So Shaun mutters (293, left margin) "*Uteralterance or the Interplay of Bones in the Womb*."

We recall *The Waste Land* and the utter alteration that takes place in the universal amniotic fluid of the sea:

> Phlebas the Phoenician, a fortnight dead, ...
> A current under sea
> Picked his bones in whispers. As he rose and fell
> He passed the stages of his age and youth
> Entering the whirlpool.

Eliot's lines may be derived from *The Tempest*, I, 2:

> Full fathom five thy father lies;
> of his bones are coral made;
> Those are pearls that were his eyes.

The Tempest provides another obvious evocation of brother rivalry and usurpation. But Shakespeare borrowed the figure of sea change from an earlier work, also a history of brother rivalry, usurpation and tyranny. In *Richard III*, I, 4, Clarence dreams of his own drowning and describes the bottom of the sea:

> Ten thousand men that fishes gnawed upon; ...
> heaps of pearl, ...
> All scattered in the bottom of the sea:
> Some lay in dead men's skulls; and in those holes
> Where eyes did once inhabit.

Eliot's "Entering the whirlpool" offers a link with Shaun's next comment: (293, left margin) "*The Vortex. Spring of Sprung Verse. The Vertex.*" The geometry problem, construction of the triangle ALP, which is prominent on this page, symbolizes the female vagina, and it seems clear that "Vortex" refers to that irresistible whirlpool. But the next words allude unmistakably to the peculiar technique of sprung verse that distinguishes the poetry of Gerard Manley Hopkins. The connection with a whirlpool and drowning at sea may be found in Hopkins's most famous poem, *The Wreck of the Deutschland.*

It should be noted that Father Hopkins, like Eliot, was a revolutionary innovator in poetry but a social and political conservative, as well as a synthesis of conflicting loyalties. An English Protestant turned Irish Jesuit, he remained intensely loyal to the English crown.

At the same time he was so subservient to Rome as to submit his poetry to his Jesuit superiors for approval. He might well be taken for a symbol of universal subjugation. And if Joyce himself is Shem, whose motto as Stephen Dedalus was (*U* 582) "*non serviam,*"[4] then Hopkins, in this respect the antithesis of Joyce, is Shaun.

This highly allusive page offers still another allusion to the Viconian cycle of rebel becoming tyrant in turn: (293.F2) "O, Laughing Sally, are we going to be toadhauntered by that old Pantifox?" Here is the Pontifex family of Samuel Butler's *The Way of All Flesh.* As a young man, Theobald Pontifex was browbeat by a tyrannical father, his one attempt at rebellion defeated. But when Theobald became a father, he attempted to impose an even more onerous tyranny on his son Ernest, whose rebellion was successful.

The foregoing allusions have been cited in detail because they put the Sherlockian allusion in proper perspective. (293.23–28) includes *The Musgrave Ritual.* The case recalls successful rebel Oliver Cromwell, whose tyranny, according to the story, literally forced the crown of England to go underground.

The Musgrave Ritual may or may not bring us back to T. S. Eliot. There is no doubt at all that for his play *Murder in the Cathedral,* Eliot borrowed eight lines (six of them verbatim) from Doyle's catechetical ritual of the Musgraves.[5] The plot of Eliot's play is thoroughly in harmony with the theme of *FW* 293, since it deals with rebellion and the conflict of authority between King Henry II and his archbishop of Canterbury, Thomas à Becket. However, the first performance of *Murder in the Cathedral* was given in London in November 1935, only four years before publication of *FW.*[6] All we can say for certain is that Joyce added *The Musgrave Ritual* lines to page 293 sometime after 1932, according to Hayman's published first-draft version of *FW.* On the other hand, T. S. Eliot is certainly present a few pages later: (305.24–25) "Thou in shanty! Thou in scanty shanty!! Thou in slanty scanty shanty!!!" The thrice repeated and increasingly emphasized "shanty" indicates the concluding line of Eliot's *Waste Land,* "*Shantih shantih shantih,*" where the spaces between the words suggest decreased emphasis, lowered voice and gradual peaceful quiescence. Joyce's amusing addition of "slanty" de-emphasizes Eliot's solemnity by including a contemporary (1932) popular song: "It's only a shanty in old shanty town,/ The roof is so slanty it touches the ground." And on the next page again we find *The Waste Land* and Eliot associated with *The Musgrave Ritual:* (306.8–9) "But while the dial are they doodling dawdling over the mugs and the grubs?" As Halper points out, this line includes winning the Dial Prize award of $2,000 for *The Waste Land.*[7] In 1937 Joyce published a limited pressrun of a handsome presentation edition, comprising a few pages from the beginning and the ending of the "Night Lessons" chapter, entitled *Storiella as She Is Syung.*[8] This edition does not include the geometry problem nor anything else from page 239, but it does include "the dial … mugs and the grubs" line.

CHAPTER 11. "TALES OF A PARKSIDE PUB" (PP. 309–382)

It is a normal, convivial night in HCE's tavern. The publican and his manservant, the Sockerson boy, are busy with the customers. Conversation flows across and along the bar, and a television set contributes other voices to the gabble. The confusion is such that it is not usually clear whether an event is actually taking place in the pub, whether it is part of a story related by the landlord or by one of the patrons or whether it is something being enacted on television. This is as it should be, for the past, present and future (the television set) merge in the eternal cycle of *FW*.

For our purpose, the most important story is the saga of the Norwegian captain which Joyce based on an anecdote remembered from his boyhood. According to Ellmann, "a hunchbacked Norwegian captain … ordered a suit from a Dublin tailor, J. H. Kerse of 34 Upper Sackville Street. The finished suit did not fit him and the captain berated the tailor for being unable to sew, whereupon the irate tailor denounced him for being impossible to fit."[9]

Joyce has embroidered the slight fabric of the captain's suit so that the captain goes sailing off on repetitious circuitous voyages. He makes the mariner a Norse raider of Ireland and a Protean Old Man of the Sea who enters the pub, runs afoul of Kersse the tailor, neglects to pay his bills and leaves with Kersse in pursuit. He returns and again bilks his creditors on leaving. But on his third visit the Viking is captured, baptized and forced to marry the landlord's daughter. His conversion to respectability brings universal joy. In one of his aspects the Norwegian captain is Olaf Tryggvesson, a fierce Viking raider who converted to Christianity, gave up piracy, married the sister of the king of Dublin and became the first Christian king of Norway. In other aspects the Norwegian captain is Proteus and Sherlock Holmes, the Norwegian named Sigerson and Captain Basil from *"Black Peter"*.

That the Norwegian captain orders a new suit of clothes may be taken as further evidence of his association with Sherlock Holmes. A change of clothing for the purpose of disguise occurs in nine of the Holmes stories cited herein. Even the horse Silver Blaze and Stapleton's Baskerville hound are disguised with paint, although these examples are not specifically mentioned in *FW*. Also, it should be recalled that *FW* refers to Holmes's "forte carlysle touch." There is no question that Holmes shared the view of Carlyle's Professor Teufelsdrockh in *Sartor Resartus* that man "by purpose and design masks himself in clothes." In fact, Joyce has twice associated Holmes with the Clothes Philosopher, in *A Scandal in Bohemia* and in *The Illustrious Client.*

The Norwegian captain's demand for new clothes is thus linked to Holmes. It may be noted further that Clive Hart confirms the identity of the Norwegian with the Sockerson boy. Says Hart: "It has generally been assumed that the Norwegian Captain is Earwicker, but it often seems more likely that he is an incarnation of Earwicker's anti-self, the Manservant."[10]

(325.27–34) "And sayd he to the nowedding captain ... comeether sayd he, my merrytime mareloup, you wutan whaal, sayd he, into the shipfolds of our quadrupede island.... And no more of your maimed acts after this with your kowtoros and criados." Here the captain is called a sea wolf (mareloup) and a whale and identified with Proteus, the herdsman who brings his footless seals to their fold on the island of Pharos (shipfolds of our quadrupede island). And Proteus is told, Don't try to escape with your cow and bull (kowtoros) miming acts! *The Man with the Twisted Lip,* who mimed being maimed, is also recalled here. The title "nowedding captain" is particularly appropriate for Sherlock Holmes, who asserted, "I shall never marry." An identification with the Sockerson boy may be seen in "criado" (Spanish, manservant).

It seems appropriate that the first Holmesian topic of conversation at the bar should be *A Scandal in Bohemia*. (310.20) "The man of Iren, thore's Curlymane." After sex, the second favorite topic would be sport. So it is that (322.1–25) Kersse the tailor comes back from the Baldoyle racetrack and tells the story of Silver Blaze. Since this is the longest chapter in *FW*, many other cases come up for discussion. Everything is relevant in HCE's taproom, including the television appearance of Butt and Taff (Bart and Tad), the Sholto twins from *The Sign of the Four*, and the repetition of the prankquean story in terms of *The Priory School*. An especially interesting narrative device might be called "The Ballad of the Sockerson Boy," which is introduced as the bar is being closed for the night: (370.30–35) "Boumce! ... The Sockerson boy ... those soulths of bauchees, ... Shatten up ship! Bouououmce!" Sockerson is bouncing the customers and shutting up shop, whereupon the debauchees begin to sing. (371.4–8) "For him had hord from fard a piping. As? Of?"

"Dour douchy was a sieguldson. He cooed that loud nor he was young. He cud bad caw nor he was gray Like wather parted from the say." The first verse, heard from afar, identifies Sigerson with Proteus, a sea god's son and a sea gull, as in *"Black Peter"*.

(371.18–20) "For be all rules of sport 'tis right That youth bedower'd to charm the night Whilst age is dumped to mind the day When wather parted from the say." It is barely possible that this second verse of the ballad alludes to *The Adventure of the Missing Three Quarter*, wherein a young athlete (sport) married a dowerless (bedower'd) girl against the wishes of his rich, miserly uncle; this is the only hint of this case in all of *FW*.

(371.30–32) "From Dancingtree till Suttonstone There's lads no lie would filch a crown To mull their sack and brew their tay With wather parted from the say." The third verse relates the tale of the ancient crown of England, retrieved from the water of the mere in a linen sack in *The Musgrave Ritual*.

(372.25–27) "His bludgeon's bruk, his drum is tore. For spuds we'll keep the hat he wore And role in clover on his clay By wather parted from the say." As a speculation, any hat might be used to store spuds, but no other hat is so well adapted for carrying spuds as is Sherlock Holmes's deerstalker—its earflaps extended and ribbons tied together. And the retired Holmes raised bees in clover-covered Sussex by the sea.[11]

(373.9–11) "The gangstairs strain and anger's up As Hosty rares the can and cup To speed the bogre's barque away O'er wather parted from the say." The fifth and final verse of the ballad reflects the chase down the Thames to recover the Agra treasure from the thieves in *The Sign of the Four*.

Despite the regular patronage of the Norwegian captain, HCE's pub is not on the Vico Road, nor near Howth on Dublin Bay. It is located in the Chapelizod area adjoining Dublin's great Phoenix Park. And we are not sure of the name of the pub, as Bernard Benstock has noted: "Even the pub called The Mullingar or the The Bristol (with the Phoenix understood) has surrogates galore in *Finnegans Wake* since *the* pub is also *all* pubs." Benstock goes on to cite a score or so other possible pub names that appear in *FW*. Not included is The Red Horse, which has at least an implied association, for this chapter is both evocative and specifically allusive to Henry Wadsworth Longfellow's long narrative poem *Tales of a Wayside Inn* (The Red Horse). More than half of the epic is devoted to the Norwegian "Musician's Tale—The Saga of King Olaf." This appears in *FW* initially on page (312.5) "And aweigh he yankered on the Norgean run," the Yankee poet and his Nordic rune. Longfellow is directly named: (347.26) "He call all feller come longa villa finish." The poet shares this line with Longaville, one of the avowed misogynists in Shakespeare's *Love's Labour's Lost*, and thus with another mysogynistic long fellow, Sherlock Holmes, the Nowedding Captain. Furthermore, Longfellow's musician is a tall, Norwegian violinist who, like Holmes, owns a Stradivarius.

Longfellow's landlord is "A man of ancient Pedigree/ ... By the name of Howe." (315.20) "Howe cools Eavybrolly!" (370.7–8) "Ungeborn yenklemen ... any old howe." When all the tales are told, Longfellow's landlord, like HCE, falls asleep snoring, and "a sound at times was heard,/ As when the distant bagpipes blow." (371.4–5) "For him had hord from fard a piping." The guests gone, the landlord is left alone. "The scattered lamps a moment gleamed,/ And the illuminated hostel seemed/ The constellation of the Bear." (382.30) "Now follow we out by Starloe!" There are many more clear Longfellow allusions in the chapter.

CHAPTER 12. MAMALUJO (PP. 383–399)

We left HCE asleep on the floor of his pub, which has now turned into a ship at sea. Mamalujo, perhaps a dream-within-a-dream, begins as a shipboard parody of Wagner's *Tristan und Isolde*. The Tristan motif suggests an element of *Liebestod* in the story of the Nowedding Captain and his Irish bride from the preceding chapter. The shipboard Tristan may therefore be another aspect of the Norwegian captain.

(383.1) "Three quarks for Muster Mark!" The three quarks represent the cry of sea gulls, flying overhead and defecating on King Mark of Cornwall. The German noun *Quark* denotes a slimy, filthy curd. A nuclear physicist, Dr. Murray Gell-Mann, borrowed the word from Joyce and used it to name a newly discovered subatomic particle with mysterious properties, currently well-known as a quark.

While King Mark is humiliated ashore, Tristan and Isolde share their ship with four non-Wagnerian fellow passengers. (384.11–14) "Old Matt Gregory and old Marcus and old Luke Tarpey: the four of us and sure ... old Johnny MacDougall." Included in these lines is a ribald drinking song, "Glorious, one keg of beer for the four of us." Their surnames are derived from *The Sign of the Four*, as has been noted. In one way or another, the Four are present on almost every page of this chapter.

It would seem that Wagner was much in Joyce's mind while he was writing Mamalujo. While the primary theme is Tristan und Isolde (388.4) "mild aunt Liza" (*Mild und leise*—the Liebestod), there may also be a reference to Elsa from *Lohengrin*. (388.6) "So mulct per wenche is Elsker woed." And there are other Wagnerian hints. (387.33–36) "And his widdy the giddy is wreathing her murmoirs" (Forest Murmurs—*Siegfried*) ... "Mind mand gunfree" (mad Kundry—*Parsifal*) by Gladeys Rayburn!" (Brunnhilde's fire-circled glade—*Die Walkure*) ... "Runtable's Reincorporated" (Wagner's reworking of Arthurian legend).

Mention of Wagner in this context is relevant to a discussion of Sherlock Holmes because *The Sign of the Four* strikes an additional Wagnerian chord. The plot of *The Sign* seems to be derived from *The Ring of the Nibelungs*. In both stories we have a stolen treasure, bringing death to its possessor and, most significantly, interfering with the fulfillment of love. The treasure is finally lost in a river.

There is a lonely heroine won in the face of obstacles and even a murderous, vindictive dwarf, eventually slain by the hero.

That Joyce admired Wagner as a dramatist is apparent in an early critical essay: "Even the least part of Wagner—his music—is beyond Bellini.... Every race has its own myths and it is in these that early drama often finds an outlet. The author of *Parsifal* has recognized this and hence his work is solid as a rock ... *Lohengrin* ... *is* not an Antwerp legend but a world drama."[12]

It is well established that Joyce began work on *FW* in 1923. A fragment was written in Paris initially, but the first complete chapter was conceived and drafted while Joyce was taking a summer holiday at Bognor, in Sussex. This first completed chapter, Mamalujo, is unique in its strong concentration of Sherlockian allusions, all to a single case. According to Ellmann, "Aside from a visit from T. S. Eliot, the sojourn at Bognor was uneventful."[13] It would seem very possible that the visit with Eliot, a strong Sherlock Holmes enthusiast, contributed to *The Sign of the Four* allusions in Mamalujo. The Wagnerian element provides a link.

In 1923 Eliot was pleased with the success of his prize-winning poem *The Waste Land*, a circumstance that, Halper has suggested, created a Shem-Shaun rivalry in Joyce's mind. Halper says that Joyce wanted to show Eliot "the way it should be done." As one example, from *The Waste Land* Joyce took Tiresias, "broken into Four Old Men," and put them in Mamalujo.[14] Did Joyce also take the Tristan theme from Eliot? In the very beginning of *The Waste Land* (lines 31–34) we find a direct quotation from the first act of the opera, the song of the seaman in the foretop:

> Frisch weht der Wind
> Der Heimat zu
> Mein Irisch Kind
> Wo weilest du?

But if Joyce wanted to beat Eliot at his own game of creative borrowing, Sherlock Holmes would offer a most appropriate theme. It is now known that Eliot inserted allusions to various Sherlock Holmes stories into five of his poetic works.[15] To those five universally recognized examples we may add a sixth, *The Waste Land*. Here is Eliot in his "Notes" to that poem: "266. The Song of the (three) Thames-daughters begins here. From line 292 to 306 inclusive they speak in turn. V. *Götterdämmerung*, III, 1: the Rhine-daughters." Joyce's Four also speak in turn, and Doyle's Four were bereft of their treasure.

In *Götterdämmerung*, III, the Rhine maidens begin by lamenting the loss of the Rhinegold. Here are the beginning lines (266–76) of the song of the Thames-daughters from *The Waste Land*:

> The river sweats
> Oil and tar
> The barges drift
> With the turning tide
> Red sails
> Wide
> To leeward, swing on the heavy spar.
> The barges wash
> Drifting logs
> Down Greenwich reach
> Past the Isle of Dogs ...

And here are certain passages from "The End of the Islander," Chapter 10 of *The Sign of the Four*. Holmes and Watson were aboard the police launch in pursuit of the launch Aurora which was carrying Jonathan Small, Tonga and the Agra treasure swiftly away down the Thames:

"We flashed past barges, steamers, merchant-vessels, in and out, behind this one and round the other ...

"We had shot through the pool, past the West India Docks, down the long Deptford Reach and up again after rounding the Isle of Dogs."

And from *The Waste Land* again, the conclusion of the song of the Thames-daughters (lines 296–310):

> My feet are at Moorgate, and my heart
> Under my feet. After the event
> ......
> On Margate Sands.
> I can connect
> Nothing with nothing.
> The broken fingernails of dirty hands.
> My people humble people who expect

Nothing.
......
O Lord Thou pluckest me out
O Lord Thou pluckest ......

In *The Sign of the Four*, when the police launch was almost within boarding stance of the *Aurora*, Small ran his craft ashore on a marshy bank:

"The fugitive sprang out, but his stump instantly sank its whole length into the sodden soil. In vain he struggled ... kicked frantically into the mud with his other foot, but his struggles only bored his wooden pin deeper into the sticky bank. When we brought our launch alongside ... we were able to haul him out and to drag him, like some evil fish, over our side."

Next in *The Waste Land* comes "IV. Death by Water" (lines 312–18)

Phlebas the Phoenician, a fortnight dead,
Forgot the cry of, gulls, and the deep sea swell
And the profit and the loss,
A current under sea
Picked his bones in whispers. . . .
Entering the whirlpool.

Just before the *Aurora* ran aground, Tonga was shot and fell overboard. Watson "caught one glimpse of his venomous, menacing eyes amid the white swirl of the waters." The body was never recovered. "Somewhere in the dark ooze at the bottom of the Thames lie the bones of that strange visitor to our shores."

One cannot flatly assert that Eliot's words, phrases and images derive from *The Sign of the Four*, deliberately and consciously, like his acknowledged use of *The Musgrave Ritual* in *Murder in the Cathedral*. The lines from *The Waste Land* are such that to venture beyond speculation is to find oneself "on the edge of a grimpen, where is no secure foothold."[16]

On the other hand, we may confidently assert that Eliot would not have been offended at the suggestion of a subconscious Sherlockian influence on his creative process. As for the association between *Götterdämmerung* and *The Sign of the Four*, that is also completely consistent with Eliot's theory of artistic creation. In fact, his appreciation of the Sherlock Holmes saga was probably enhanced by his recognition of mythological roots in some of the cases.

Finally, another of Eliot's "Notes" (line 218) indicates that in *The Waste Land* he used a technique of merging identities similar to that used by Joyce in *FW*, "218 Tiresias . . . melts into the Phoenician Sailor, and the latter is not wholly distinct from Ferdinand Prince of Naples."[17]

NOTES

1. James S. Atherton, *The Books at the Wake* (New York: Viking Press, 1960), 37.

2. Sir Herbert Read, quoted in Allen Tate, ed., *T. S. Eliot—The Man and His Work* (New York: Dell Publishing, 1966), 26.

3. William York Tindall, *A Reader's Guide to Finnegans Wake* (New York: Farrar, Strauss and Giroux, 1969), 181–82; Nathan Halper, "Joyce and Eliot: A Tale of Shem and Shaun," *The Nation*, May 1, 1965, 590–94: "Joyce declared himself a Shem; he made Eliot a Shaun ... In every field of activity, what the rebel has created becomes the Church, the State, the Academy.

4. Cf. Joyce, *A Portrait of the Artist as a Young Man* (New York: Compass, 1956), 239.

5. T. S. Eliot, *Murder in the Cathedral* (Thomas à Becket and the Second Tempter):

> THOMAS: Whose was it:
> TEMPTER: His who is gone.
> THOMAS: Who shall have it:
> TEMPTER: He who will come. ...
> THOMAS: What shall we give for it: ...
> THOMAS: Why should we give it:

6. David Hayman, *A First Draft Version of Finnegans Wake* (Austin: University of Texas Press, 1963), 31–33.

7. Halper, "Joyce and Eliot."

8. Joyce, *Storiella as She Is Syung* (London: Corvinus Press, 1937) n. p.

9. Richard Ellmann, *James Joyce* (New York: Oxford University Press, 1959), 22.

10. Clive Hart, *Structure and Motif in Finnegans Wake* (Evanston, Ill.: Northwestern University Press, 1962), 125.

11. Cf. Oliver Goldsmith, *She Stoops to Conquer*. 1, 2: An Ale-house. "what, though I am obligated to dance a bear.... May this be my poison if my bear ever dances but to the very genteelest of tunes. *Water Parted* or the minuet in *Ariadne*."

12. James Joyce, *The Critical Writings* . ed. Ellsworth Mason and Richard Ellmann (New York: Viking Press, 1964), 40, 43, 44.

13. Ellmann, *Joyce*, 567.

14. Halper, "*Joyce* and Eliot."

15. Eliot, *Murder in the Cathedral*, noted above. Also: "Macavity the Mystery Cat" is Professor Moriarty. "Gus the Theatre Cat" played the role of Tiger hunted by Colonel Sebastian Moran. "Ralph Hodgson Esqre" owned a Baskerville Hound. "East Coker" alludes to the Grimpen Mire also from *The Hound of the Baskervilles*.

16. Eliot, "East Coker."

17. Atherton has compared Joyce's technique of merging identities in FW to superimposing numerous photoportrait negatives of different individuals and printing thc result. *The Books at the Wake* (New York: Viking Press, 1960), 23.

Chapter 19

Motif and Leitmotif (III, 13–16. IV, 17)

CHAPTER 13. SHAUN THE POSTMAN (PP. 403–28)

In a letter to the wealthy Englishwoman Harriet Shaw Weaver, who was his patron, Joyce described Shaun in this chapter as a "barrel rolling down the river Liffey."[1] Perhaps Miss Weaver understood this, as well as another letter referring to Shaun as a "man of four watches."[2]

In his capacity as a postman, Shaun delivers a letter, presumably the one from Boston, (413.3–4) "To the Very Honourable The Memory of Disgrace, the Most Noble, Sometime Sweepyard at the Service of the Writer." Subsequently Shaun declines an invitation to sing but instead relates his version of Aesop's fable of the Ant and the Grasshopper. Shaun himself is the virtuous Ant and his scapegrace brother, Shem, is the Grasshopper. "The Ondt and the Gracehoper" (414.19–419.8) is certainly one of the funniest passages in *FW*. The chapter makes no detectable allusions to Sherlock Holmes.

CHAPTER 14. JAUN THE LADYKILLER (PP. 429–73)

Shaun as Don Juan, (430.32–33) "the killingest ladykiller all by kindness, now you Jaun," lectures twenty-nine leap-year girl students at St. Bride's Academy. He is supported by a (429.19–21) "butterblond warden of the peace, one comestabulish Sigurdsen, … exsearfaceman … bootblacked." Apparently this is Holmes disguised with burnt cork (searface) or boot polish.[3] The subject of Jaun's sermon is sexual morality. He mentions (449.10–11) "the nippy girl of my heart's appointment, ... Ipostila, my Lady of Lyons." This is the seduced Mrs. Laura Lyons, who posted a letter making an appointment with the murdered Sir Charles Baskerville. (450.32) "Bryony O'Bryony, thy name is Belladama!" This is Irene Adler, who lived in Briony Lodge, St. John's Wood. To Sherlock Holmes she was always *the* woman. She may appear again: (469.19–20) "The brine's my bride to be," and she is specifically named: (471.1) "Irine! Areinette!" Named on the same page is (471.30) "Sickerson, that borne of bjoerne, la garde auxiliare."

CHAPTER 15. IN QUEST OF YAWN (PP. 474–554)

Chapter 11 concluded with HCE in a drunken sleep on the floor of his pub, raising the possibility that the Mamalujo chapter which follows may be HCE's dream. The same thing now happens to Shaun. (474.1) "Pure Yawn lay low, On the mead of the hillock lay." And once again the Four Old Men appear (475.18–19) "to hold their sworn star chamber quiry on him." Drunk or sober, Yawn is in a trance–like state and able to answer questions. Thus the inquest takes on the semblance of the spiritualistic seance (498.8–499.3) attended by Professor Challenger in Doyle's novel *The Land of Mist.*[4] However, the Four Judges soon finish with Yawn and interrogate other witnesses on other matters. Touched on in passing is the case of Oscar Slater, wrongfully accused of murder with a hammer. (511.4) "With Slater's hammer perhaps?" On (517.2–23) there is intensive questioning concerning the events at Reichenbach Falls. On the next page (518.15–18) Colonel Sebastian Moran's air gun is offered as an exhibit. And on (530.17–22) "Sickerson the lizzyboy" is recalled as an expert witness on ALP's Mamafesta. Next (534.1–36), we find testimony concerning *The Stock-Broker's Clerk* which includes the fact that "Sherlook is lorking for him." The inquest concludes (599.10) with an incantation of the names of the Four: "Mattahah! Marahah! Luahah! Johanahanhana!" The pseudo-Sanskrit sounds are probably a parody of the concluding "Shantih shantih shantih" of Eliot's *The Waste Land*.

CHAPTER 16. AND SO TO BED (PP. 555–590)

Meanwhile, back at the inn, HCE is still stretched out on the floor. Kate, the housekeeper, hearing a knocking noise, comes down and helps him up to bed. Shortly thereafter the cry of a child awakens him, and he rises to investigate. He looks in on his sleeping daughter, and (556.16) "Isobel, she is so pretty, truth to tell," that he becomes sexually aroused and stumbles back to bed. In his troubled sleep he dreams that the Four Old Men invade his bedroom, making notes of his misbehavior, and accompanied by Soakersoon the constable. (566.8–10) "The four seneschals ... sharping up their penisills. The boufcither Soakersoon at holdup tent sticker" (boufcither equals bullfighter?). HCE now appears in court on trial for incest before a jury, (574.31–32) "a sour dozen of stout fellows all of whom were curiously named after doyles." There is also a witness, (575.6–7) "Ann Doyle, 2 Coppinger's Cottages, the Doyle's country." The witness made a proposal that (575.32) "was ruled out on appeal by Judge JeremyDoyler."

HCE stirs in his sleep and the dream is interrupted. The house settles down, so that later, when (586.28) "pollysigh patrolman Seekersenn" passes by, he finds that all is well. Several passages on these pages suggest *The Adventure of the Speckled Band.*

CHAPTER 17. SOFT MORNING CITY (PP. 593–628)

Whereas Chapter 15 concluded with an invocation in pseudo-Sanskrit, the final chapter begins with an invocation in authentic Sanskrit: (593.1) "Sandhyas! Sandhyas! Sandhyas!" In this context the word means "daybreak." The chapter is a soliloquy—Anna Livia Plurabelle personifying the River Liffey. Her source is a rain cloud: (593.19) "A hand from the cloud emerges, holding a chart expanded." So the Liffey flows through the Irish countryside and the city of Dublin to the bay and the open sea. There the water will evaporate, becoming cloud, and the cycle will begin again. ALP's memories include some of the adventures of Sherlock Holmes in short takes: (595.34–36 and 599.4–8) *The Priory School*; (607.28–608.1–11) *The Norwood Builder* and the bloody thumbprint noted by "Sigurd Sigerson ... bledprusshers"; (622.25) *"Black Peter"*. (617.14–15) "Conan Boyles will pudge the daylives out through him" alludes to Conan Doyle's well-known passion for boxing.[5]

(619.19) "Soft morning, city! Lsp! I am leafy speafing." So begins the beginning of the final words of *FW*. These ten pages include some of the most melodious lyrical prose in English literature. The meanings may be diffused, as seen through a morning mist, but the breathtaking quality of the imagery is inescapable.

(628.1–4) "I go back to you, my cold father, my cold mad father, my cold mad feary father, till the near sight of the mere size of him, the moyles and moyles of it, moananoaning, makes me seasilt saltsick and I rush, my only, into your arms."

In his poem "The Triumph of Time" Swinburne used a similar image.

> I will go back to the great sweet mother,
> Mother and lover of men, the sea.
> I will go down to her, I and no other,
> Close with her, kiss her and mix her with me;
> Cling to her, strive with her, hold her fast.

But in another poem, "The Garden of Proserpine," Swinburne gave voice to a thought totally antithetical to *FW*.

> That no life lives forever;
> That dead men rise up never;
> That even the weariest river
> Winds somewhere safe to sea.

In Joyce's book all life lives forever: (628.14–16) "Finn, again! Take. Bussoftlhee, mememormee! Till thousendsthee. Lps. The keys to. Given! A way a lone a last a loved a long the" There is no period because the sentence is continued on the first page of the text (3.1) "riverrun, past Eve and Adam's from swerve of shore to bend ... "

NOTES

1. James Joyce to Harriet Shaw Weaver, May 1924, *Letters* I, ed. Stuart Gilbert (New York: Viking Press, 1957), 214.

2. James Joyce to Harriet Shaw Weaver, April 1926, *Letters* III, ed. Richard Ellmann (New York: Viking Press, 1966), 140.

3. Cf. (517.17) "Did Box then try to shine his puss?" Also (315.9) "Burniface, shiply efter" - the Norwegian Captain.

4. See Chapter 1, "It Seems There Were Two Irishman," page 4, of this book.

5. Arthur Conan Doyle, *Memories and Adventures* (Boston: Little, Brown, 1924), 265–268.

Chapter 20

And Watsy Lyke Sees after All Rinsings

Vico had put forward a theory of history in which he contended that human societies originate, develop and reach their end according to fixed laws of rotation, moving, or rather rotating in similar cycles. Further, this theory was to be deduced not from a review of chronologically-arranged historical events (inferring them to be unconnected phenomena) but from the lives, actual or legendary, of race heroes, that is, personalities that become in themselves mass-personalities; for what, after all, is the race hero but the visible symbol of the heroic consciousness of the race.[1]

Thus wrote Herbert Gorman, Joyce's first biographer, in discussing the influence of Giovanni Battista Vico on the structure of *FW*. Whether or not Gorman's reading of Viconian theory is adequate, it cannot be denied that *FW* alludes to "the lives, actual or legendary, of race heroes." Furthermore, Sherlock Holmes obviously qualifies as a race hero, a "mass-personality." Within the lifetime of his creator Sherlock had passed from the realm of fiction into the realm of legend. And although the effect of the legendary detective on the development of society may have been so intangible as to be judged negligible, Holmes shared Vico's belief in the cyclical nature of history. "Everything comes in circles, even Professor Moriarty," stated Holmes in *The Valley of Fear*.

While Joyce accorded some recognition to the Shem side of Holmes's personality, his purpose in *FW* was better served by identifying the detective primarily as a policeman, a "comestabulish." He chose to minimize an essential aspect of Holmes the race hero, which is that Holmes is less an upholder of the Law than an upholder of Justice. Sometimes he is a law unto himself. This Robin Hood aspect of his hero is central to Doyle's concept. Holmes is never a "Scotland Yard Jack-in-Office."

In his essay "Baker Street to Eccles Street," Hugh Kenner equates Holmes with Stephen Dedalus as an "anarchic aesthete" and observes: "In about half his cases Holmes as judge supplements the work of Holmes the sleuth in permitting the criminal to escape."[2] Although Kenner probably exaggerates Holmes's leniency, the point is well made. "I am not retained by the police to supply their deficiencies," said Holmes in *The Adventure of the Blue Carbuncle*.

As Kenner goes on to suggest, Doyle's own personality was compounded almost equally of Shem and Shaun characteristics. He was a loyal subject of the crown and a defender of the empire. At the same time he was strongly attached to the tradition of chivalry and was always ready, if he saw cause, to espouse the unpopular or the unconventional. Doyle as the champion of the underdog and liberator of Oscar Slater was recognized by Joyce in the same *FW* passage that acknowledges the high literary quality of the Sherlock Holmes stories as compared to other detective fiction: (165.31–36) "I should like to ask that Shedlock Holmes person who is out for raising the roofs of our criminal classics ... unless he happens of himself, *movible tectu*, to have a slade off."

There is, of course, no doubt whatever that Holmes qualifies for participation in the great *FW* theme of Fall, Death and Resurrection because of circumstances totally unrelated to artistic design. And Joyce recognized the possibility of fortuitous creation. "If a man hacking in fury at a block of wood make there an image of a cow (say) has he made a work of art?" Joyce asked himself in his notebook.[3]

Other nuances of Doyle's work are not so plainly fortuitous. Did Doyle knowingly stretch the thread of Ariadne through the Great Grimpen Mire? Was he aware that the Agra treasure, lost in the Thames, was once owned by the Rhine maidens? Did he recognize Proteus in Holmes and the Phoenix in Jonas Oldacre? We note Gorman's comment on the blossoming of *FW* in Sussex: "Who would attempt to say from what particular seed it flowered? Or from how many? These are the mysteries of creation and any discussion of them is always nine parts assumption."[4] The observation might well apply to Doyle.

In any case, Doyle was unawed by his achievement in creating a modern legend and would willingly have traded his race hero's immortality for a like amount of contemporary fame for himself. In 1927, three years before his death, he could write in his preface to *The Case Book of Sherlock Holmes*:

> I had fully determined at the conclusion of *The Memoirs* to bring Holmes to an end.... I did the deed, but fortunately no coroner had pronounced upon the remains, and so, after a long interval, it was not difficult for me to respond to the flattering demand and to explain my rash act away. I have never regretted it, for I have not in actual practice found that these lighter sketches have prevented me from exploring and finding my limitations in such varied branches of literature as history, poetry, historical novels, psychic research and the drama. Had Holmes never existed I could not have done more, although he may perhaps have stood a little in the way of the recognition of my more serious literary work.
>
> And so, reader, farewell to Sherlock Holmes!

On the final page of Chapter 16 of *FW* (590.4–18), with HCE settled down in bed, occurs a passage that might be read as a parody, if not a paraphrase, of this valediction by Doyle to Sherlock Holmes:

> Pepep. Pay bearer, sure and sorry, at foot of ohoho honest policist. On never again, by Phoenis, swore on him Lloyd's.... They knew him, the covenanter, by rote at least, for a chameleon at last, in his true falseheaven colours from ultraviolent to subred tissues. That's his last tryon to march through the grand tryomphal arch. His reignbolt's shot. Never again! ...
>
> Agreed, Wu Welsher, he was chogfulled to beacsate on earn as in hiving, of foxold conningnesses but who, hey honey, for all values of his latters, integer intergerrimost, was the foremast of the firm? At folkmood hailed, at part farwailed, accwmwladed concloud, Nuah-Nuah, Nebob of Nephilim! After all, what followed for apprentice sake?

If we were to read these two paragraphs in Sherlockian terms, we should note initially that the concluding story in the first edition of *The Case Book of Sherlock Holmes* is a murder case entitled *The Adventure of the Retired Colourman* (his true falseheaven colours from ultraviolent to subred tissues....His reignbolt's shot. Never again!). Then we should note that Joyce seems to make ironic reference to the financial success of the Holmes stories, which he compares to an insurance company annuity, payable after the death of the insured, "at foot of ohoho honest policist."

However, the paragraph (590.4–12) " Pepep ... Never again!" appears in David Hayman's *First Draft Version of Finnegans Wake*, and was apparently written by Joyce not later than 1925.[5] Therefore, despite the coincidence of "colours from ultraviolent" and "retired colourman," the initial inspiration for Joyce's lines could not have been Doyle's valediction for Sherlock Holmes, since *The Case Book* was not published until 1927.

That does not rule out the possibility that Joyce recognized the relevance later and added the next paragraph (590.13–19) which begins, "Agreed, Wu Welsher ...," which is not in the *First Draft Version*. The possibility is strengthened by the change from "honest policy" in the *First Draft* to "honest policist," with the added connotation of policeman, in the final version (590.5).

We next observe (590.13–18) that the "Welsher" word *cwm* means a valley or a ravine with a stream at the bottom. Hence "accwmwladed" equals lay dead in a *cwm*, as at Reichenbach, a fate widely "farwailed." We regret that Joyce may have stooped to using the scurrilous Sassenach slander "Welsher" to imply that Doyle somehow reneged in bringing Holmes back to life. *Conan* Doyle himself appears in "conningnesses" and perhaps in "Nebob of Nephilim," his cloudy, necrophilic obsession with spiritualism. As for Doyle's evaluation of Sherlock Holmes as "lighter sketches" compared to "poetry, historical novels, psychic research and the drama," Joyce properly scoffs at these later aspirations as "what followed for apprentice sake."

Finally, there is also an allusion to the retired Holmes as a bee keeper (earn as in hiving ... hey honey). In the leisured ease of his retirement (*His Last Bow*) Holmes produced an authoritative work, *Practical Handbook of Bee Culture, with some Observations upon the Segregation of the Queen*. The title is suggested in *FW* at the bottom of the page: (590.27–28) "While the queenbee he staggerhorned blesses her bliss."

The acid remarks of Holmes to Watson sometimes took a particular form which provides a final pair of parallel quotations for a summation of this study. From *The Adventure of the Dancing Men*:

" 'How absurdly simple!' I cried.

" 'Quite so!' said he, a little nettled. 'Every problem becomes very childish when once it is explained to you.' "

(245.33–34) "And Watsy Lyke sees after all rinsings and don't omiss Kate, homeswab homely, put in with the bricks."

Finnegans Wake is, among other things, the most perplexing whodunit ever written. (628.15) "The keys to. Given!" said Joyce on the next-to-the-last line on the last page before the begin-again.

NOTES

1. Herbert Gorman, *James Joyce* (New York: Farrar and Rhinehart, 1939), 332.

2. Hugh Kenner, "Baker Street to Eccles Street" in *Dublin's Joyce* (Boston: Beacon Press, 1956), 158-78.

3. James Joyce, "Aesthetics" in *Critical Writings* (New York: Viking Press, 1964) 146. Cf. *A Portrait of the Artist as a Young Man* (New York: Compass, 1956), 214.

4. Gorman, op. cit.

5. David Hayman, *A First Draft Version of Finnegans Wake* (Austin: University of Texas Press, 1963), 324.

Bibliography

Atherton, James S. *The Books at the Wake*. New York: Viking Press, 1960.

Blyth, Henry. *The Rakes*. New York: Dial Press, 1971.

Budgen, Frank. *James Joyce and the Making of Ulysses*. Oxford: Oxford University Press, 1972.

Butcher, S. H., and Andrew Land. *The Odyssey of Homer—Done into English Prose*. New York: Modern Library, n.d.

Campbell, Joseph, and Henry Morton Robinson. *A Skeleton Key to Finnegans Wake*. New York: Viking Press, 1961.

Carr, John Dickson. *The Life of Sir Arthur Conan Doyle*. New York: Harper and Brothers, 1949.

Doyle, Arthur Conan. *Conan Doyle's Best Books*. New York: P. F. Collier and Son, n.d.

———. *Memories and Adventures: The Autobiography of Sir Arthur Conan Doyle*. Boston: Little, Brown, 1923.

———. *The Stark-Munro Letters*. New York: D. Appleton, 1895.

Eliot, T. S. *Collected Poems, 1909–1962*. New York: Harcourt Brace, 1964.

Ellmann, Richard. *James Joyce*. New York: Oxford University Press, 1959.

Famous Ghost Stories. New York: Illustrated Modern Library, 1944.

Frazer, James George. *The New Golden Bough*. Edited by Theodor H. Gaster. New York: New American Library, 1959.

Gilbert, Stuart. *James Joyce's Ulysses*. New York: Modern Library, 1952.

Glasheen, Adaline. *A Census of Finnegans Wake*. Evanston, Ill.: Northwestern University Press.

———. *A Second Census of Finnegans Wake*. Evanston, Ill.: Northwestern University Press, 1963.

Gorman, Herbert. *James Joyce*. New York: Farrar and Rhinehart, 1939.

Graves, Robert. *The White Goddess.* New York: Vintage Books, 1958.

Halper, Nathan. "Joyce and Eliot: A Tale of Shem and Shaun." *The Nation,* May 1, 1965.

Hart, Clive. *Structure and Motif in Finnegans Wake.* Evanston, Ill.: Northwestern University Press, 1962.

Hayman, David. *A First Draft Version of Finnegans Wake.* Austin: University of Texas Press, 1963.

Hodgart, Matthew J. C. "Shakespeare and *Finnegans Wake.*" *The Cambridge Journal* 6 (September 1953).

Jenkins, William D. "From a Drop of Water, an Atlantic, a Niagara ..., From a Pebble, the Universe." *Baker Street Journal* 25, no. 3 (September 1975).

———. "Have Sight of Proteus: Mythological Archetypes in the Sherlockian Canon." *Baker Street Journal* 34, no. 3 (September 1984).

Joyce, James. *The Critical Writings.* Edited by Ellsworth Mason and Richard Ellmann. New York: Viking Press, 1964.

———. *Finnegans Wake.* London: Faber and Faber, 1939; New York: Viking Press, 1939.

———. *Letters* 1. Edited by Stuart Gilbert. New York: Viking Press, 1957.

———. *Letters* 3. Edited by Richard Ellmann. New York: Viking Press, 1966.

———. *A Portrait of the Artist as a Young Man.* Reprint. New York: Compass, 1963.

———. *Stephen Hero.* Reprint. Norfolk, Conn.: New Directions, 1963.

———. *Storiella as She Is Syung.* London: Corvinus Press, 1937.

———. *Ulysses.* Reprint. New York: Random House/Modern Library, 1961.

Joyce, Stanislaus. *My Brother's Keeper.* New York: Viking Press, 1958.

Kaufmann, Walter. *Existentialism from Dostoevsky to Sartre.* New York: Meridian Books, 1956.

Kenner, Hugh. *Dublin's Joyce.* Boston: Beacon Press, 1962.

Nordon, Pierre. *Conan Doyle: A Biography.* New York: Holt, Rhinehart and Winston, 1964.

Pearson, Kesketh. *Conan Doyle,* New York, 1960.
Plato, *Phaido*. Translated by Benjamin Jowett.
Senn, Fritz. "Carey Was His Name." *James Joyce Quarterly* 24 (Winter 1987).
Tate, Allen, ed. *T. S. Eliot—The Man and His Work.* New York: Dell Publishing, 1966.
Tindall, William York. *A Reader's Guide to Finnegans Wake.* New York: Farrar, Strauss and Giroux, 1969.
———. *A Reader's Guide to James Joyce.* New York, 1964.
Wilson, Edmund. "The Dream of H. C. Earwicker." In *The Wound and the Bow.* New York: Oxford University Press, 1965.

Index

Q

R

S

T

V

W

Y

Z

About the Author

WILLIAM D. JENKINS was an independent researcher who specialized in late 19th- and early 20th-century literature. His work was published in such journals as *Studies in Philology*, *Modern Fiction Studies*, *James Joyce Quarterly*, and the *Baker Street Journal*.

ingramcontent.com/pod-product-compliance
ng Source LLC
burg PA
941310726
0001B/10